NEST OF VIPERS

Nest of Vipers
Peter Cave

MAINSTREAM
PUBLISHING

EDINBURGH AND LONDON

Copyright © Peter Cave, 1993

From the series written by Glenn Chandler
Producer   Robert Love
Director   Graham Theakston

First published in Great Britain in 1993 by
MAINSTREAM PUBLISHING COMPANY (EDINBURGH) LTD
7 Albany Street
Edinburgh EH1 3UG

ISBN 1 85158 555 9

A catalogue record for this book is available from the British
Library

Typeset in 11/12 Garamond by WEPS, Cockenzie, East Lothian,
Scotland

Printed in Great Britain by BPCC Wheatons, Exeter

Chapter One

The New Link Road project had been the subject of major controversy from the first day it was mooted by the Department of Transport.

Many Glasgow residents complained bitterly that Whitehall ought to be picking up a bigger slice of the tab, and there were allegations that City Council members had taken backhanders from contractors tendering for the job.

Then the environmentalists had got in on the act, bemoaning yet further loss of precious but ever-dwindling green belt which encircled the 'Dear Green Place', as some older Glaswegians still referred to their beloved city. Their argument was further strengthened by the fact that parts of the planned route were less than half a mile away from one of the most important archaeological sites discovered in Scotland for over the past six decades. What appeared to be a major Roman encampment had been unearthed, and had already yielded up a wealth of scientific treasures. At one stage, it had looked as though the Greens might win the day.

But the planners got their way in the end. The contracts were awarded, work started, and the entire subject had ceased to make headlines in the local newspapers.

Until now, it seemed. The Link Road scheme still had a few surprises up its sleeve.

Detective Chief Inspector Jim Taggart didn't normally bother himself much with local politics. For a start he didn't have the time, and he had more or less got used to his wife Jean being the social conscience for both of them. He was, on the other hand, very much bothered when human skulls started popping out of the ground.

DS Mike Jardine pulled the car to a halt well clear of the construction site. Switching off the engine, he climbed out and waited for Taggart to join him before starting to walk towards a small knot of people clustered around the shovel of one of the mechanical diggers.

Taggart moodily reviewed the sea of mud and ploughed earth all around him, his eyes following the line of the road excavations as it snaked like an ugly black scar across previously green fields.

'I used to pick blackberries up here when I was a boy,' he muttered, managing to make the simple statement sound like a total rejection of all progress since puberty.

This information, and any significance it might have had, went over the top of Jardine's head. He was already locked securely into his 'on the job' mode. The construction site was simply the scene of a grisly discovery, possibly a crime.

'Of course, it could turn out to be another one of those Roman skulls, sir. The archaeological dig where they turned up the other two is just over the hill there.' Jardine pointed vaguely beyond the cluster of building huts and machinery.

Taggart merely grunted. He led the way to where City Pathologist Dr Andrews was examining the contents of a mechanical shovel.

Andrews looked up, briefly, nodding by way of greeting. 'I'm afraid the press got here before you,' he announced. 'They practically followed me out here. But then I suppose skulls are flavour of the month at the moment.'

Taggart glanced across towards the group of reporters and photographers being kept at bay by a handful of uniformed officers and a few strands of yellow tape. He noted, with faint satisfaction, that DC Jackie Reid seemed to have taken charge of the operation. Although Taggart would never have allowed her or Jardine to know it, he was developing a growing respect for the dedicated young officer.

Satisfied that the gentlemen of the press seemed to be under control, he turned his attention back to Andrews and the contents of the shovel. There, nesting on top of a pile of freshly dug earth like some obscene egg, lay a badly damaged but clearly recognisable human skull.

Taggart sighed. 'Let's have some good news,' he said to Andrews. 'Tell us it's *I Claudius* and we can all go home for breakfast.'

Andrews shook his head almost apologetically. 'I think breakfast is going to be here. The Romans cremated most of their dead.'

'Then what about the two skulls they found last month?' Jardine put in. 'They were whole.'

Dr Andrews frowned slightly, as though he was unused to having his statements questioned.

'They were the exception. That's why the archaeologists are having such a field day.'

As though dismissing the junior officer completely, Andrews returned his full attention to Taggart.

'I'd say this one has had its teeth removed and the jawbone smashed deliberately.'

Taggart was about to reflect upon the significance of this information when a sudden whoop of excitement from one of the site workers distracted his attention. About twenty yards away, a digger had found another skull, and was waving it in the air above his head.

A buzz of excitement broke out amongst the group of news-papermen.

'Look, he's got another one,' someone called out — and it seemed to act like a trigger for mob action. Suddenly the nice orderly police control operation was in chaos as they all ducked under the tapes and stampeded towards the jubilant workman like a flock of startled sheep.

Unused to such attention, the workman froze as the news-hounds closed in upon him. He grinned stupidly, holding the skull in his hand.

'That's right. Look as though you're pleased to see it,' called out one of the press photographers, lining up his camera for a shot. The bemused workman held the skull out at arm's length, leering at it like some ham actor performing the 'Alas, poor Yorick' scene from a production of *Hamlet*.

Taggart groaned, and was just about to make a dash towards the scene when he noticed DC Reid had already moved in to restore control. Pushing through the excited newsmen, she snatched the skull from the workman's hands.

'I'll take that, if you don't mind.'

Bearing it like a trophy, she carried it across to Taggart, looking pleased with herself. 'Sir, one of the truck drivers just found this.'

If she was expecting praise, she didn't get it. Taggart scowled at her. 'Why didn't you leave it where it was?'

Jackie Reid looked crestfallen. 'Sir, he already had it in his hand,' she protested. 'He was posing with it for photographs.'

Taggart controlled his annoyance with an effort. The girl was right to protest. It wasn't her fault that a valuable piece of evidence had been removed from its original burial place. 'Well, just put it down,' he muttered, his tone softening.

DC Reid placed the skull gently at his feet and backed away. Her eyes caught Jardine's, and she grinned. 'I was going to play football with it,' she whispered, in passing.

Jardine smiled quickly, establishing a rapport with a fellow officer. He resumed an official, businesslike look as Dr Andrews came over to join them. The three of them crouched down to look at the skull more closely.

'It looks just like the first one,' Jardine observed.

Andrews nodded, poking the skull gently with a specimen tab.

'Almost exactly the same,' he agreed. 'Teeth removed and the jawbone smashed.' He rose to his feet, turning to Taggart. 'You realise what we have here, don't you? This is somebody's private graveyard.'

'No chance that they're Roman relics — like those discovered earlier?'

Andrews shrugged. 'Possible, but I doubt it. Of course I can't be sure until I've had a chance to examine them in the lab, but I'd say these were comparatively recent.'

'Guess?' Taggart prompted.

Andrews smiled thinly. 'You know me better than that, Jim. No, you'll have to wait for facts, not speculation.'

Chapter Two

There was an ominous hissing sound, like steam escaping from a pressure valve, as Christine Gray stepped through the security doors into the venom extraction laboratory of Casco Pharmaceuticals. Although the sound was by now familiar to her, it never ceased to cause an involuntary shudder.

Dr Nielson was already taking the top off one of the reptile tanks containing a large puff adder. Holding a pair of tongs at arm's length, he gripped the deadly snake just behind the head and lifted it clear of the tank.

As though sensing that one of their fellow creatures was in some sort of danger, the rest of the snakes hissed in unison — the sound which Christine had heard.

She watched Nielson as he carried the Puff Adder to a petri dish covered with a thin rubber membrane. Pushing the snake's fangs through the rubber, Nielson loosened his grip on the tongs slightly, allowing it to bite. A trickle of viscous fluid from the reptile's hollow fangs dribbled down the inside of the glass.

Satisfied that the snake had released its full charge of venom, Nielson returned it to its tank and replaced the cover. Christine sealed the petri dish, labelled it and carried it over to a large storage refrigerator, filing it away in the correct section and making an entry on the inventory clipped to the inside of the door. She closed the refrigerator, turning back to Dr Nielson. 'Is that the last one?'

Nielson nodded. 'That's it for today. I've already milked the cobras and Black Mambas, and they're all tabbed and stored.'

Christine shuddered again. 'They don't bother you, do they?'

'Snakes? No, not really,' Nielson answered, smiling faintly. 'I've got used to them now. Little marvels of nature, really.'

Christine made a grimace of distaste. 'Little horrors, more like. I'll never get used to them.'

Nielson smiled warmly. 'Well, it doesn't prevent you from doing your job extremely efficiently, Christine. Anyway, if your own project succeeds, we won't have to go through this every month. So let's hope that you make that breakthrough soon.'

Christine shook her head. 'I think it's a long way off yet,' she said, modestly.

'Well, when it does — you just make sure that you get the credit for it, that's all,' Nielson told her. 'There are too many discoveries in this company that our esteemed director of research has taken credit for.'

'You don't like her, do you?' Christine asked.

Nielson grinned, uncharacteristically. 'About as much as you like snakes.'

The telephone rang in the main lab outside. Christine went to answer it automatically, even though she knew the call was unlikely to be for her. Although she was a scientist in her own right, she had an almost slavish devotion to Nielson, often acting more like his personal secretary than his assistant.

The call was, indeed, for Nielson. Christine waved the phone in the air, calling through the glass partitioning of the herpetarium. 'Dr Nielson, there's a woman on the phone for you. A Miss Cramer. She won't say what it's about. Personal and confidential, she says.'

Nielson cast a last glance around the herpetarium, checking that all the tanks were secured. He stepped through the security door, punching out the locking code on the electronic control console.

He took the receiver from Christine's hand as she went back to her own work bench and bent over the microscope on top of it.

'Yes, this is Dr Nielson.'

Christine eyed him covertly over her microscope, curious about the possible identity of the mystery woman. She knew the distinctive and somewhat cultured Edinburgh accent of his wife, Morag — and the caller had most certainly not been her. North of England, at a guess. It was the first time Christine had known Nielson to receive a call from a woman outside the company, and the possibilities intrigued her.

Whatever the woman's message, it seemed to take Nielson aback. His voice had a distinct stutter as he responded to her opening speech.

'I . . . I had no idea,' he said nervously. He glanced round anxiously, as though to check if anyone was listening to his conversation. 'Look, I obviously can't discuss this over the telephone,' he carried on, dropping his voice to little more than a whisper. 'I could meet you later this afternoon, if you like.'

After listening for a few more seconds, Nielson replaced the receiver. There was an odd look on his face, Christine noticed. Like a schoolboy who has been caught at the biscuit jar. He seemed a little shaken.

'Everything all right, Dr Nielson?' Christine enquired solicitously.

The man recovered himself. 'Yes . . . fine.' He paused uncertainly. 'Look, I have to go out rather unexpectedly. If anyone asks, I don't feel well. I'll be back in the morning.'

Nielson stripped off his white lab coat and retrieved his jacket from the hook on the back of the door. He left without another word, leaving Christine staring after him with a puzzled expression on her face.

Stepping through the revolving doors of the luxury Plaza East Hotel, Nielson glanced around uncertainly, a little thrown by the unaccustomed opulence of his surroundings. The hotel lounge was laid out with armchairs and small tables, obviously designed for informal business meetings.

An extremely smart young woman rose from one of the tables as he approached, obviously recognising him.

'Ah, Dr Nielson. So glad you could come. I'm Jill Cramer, of Management Quest.' She held out her hand for a formal handshake. 'Would you like a drink?' she asked, making a discreet but commanding gesture to a passing waiter, who responded immediately.

Nielson glanced at the silver serving-tray, and the crisp white bar towel draped over the waiter's arm. It seemed almost sacrilegious to desecrate it with a pint glass, but he was not a spirit drinker. And he was an invited guest, Nielson reminded himself. 'Thanks. I'll have a pint of heavy.'

Jill Cramer smiled sweetly at the waiter. 'Another mineral water for me, please.'

The waiter scurried off. There was a momentary silence, which Nielson finally broke with a facetious comment. 'You drink dangerously.'

Jill Cramer smiled, as though it was the greatest piece of witty repartee she had heard in ages. 'No, I *drive* dangerously, which is why I only drink mineral water,' she responded. She gestured to a pair of comfortable armchairs. 'Shall we sit down?'

It was as much a command as an invitation. Nielson sat down, a little overawed by the woman's undeniable power. 'So, you're what they call a headhunter in the business.'

Miss Cramer became at once a model of businesslike efficiency. 'Shall we get straight down to the point? Landsberg Chemicals in Liverpool are looking for a toxicologist of your qualifications, and I have been briefed . . .'

'Toxinologist,' Nielson interrupted her.

'I'm sorry?'

Just for a fraction of a second, the woman was thrown. It gave Nielson a moment of inner satisfaction.

'I'm a toxinologist. I work with natural toxins as distinct from toxic substances and chemicals.'

14

'Ah.' Miss Cramer nodded, still a little off balance.

Nielson pressed home his unexpected advantage. 'So, our biggest competitor wants to poach me. Is that it?' He was beginning to enjoy himself for the first time since the meeting had started. 'I take it they've made some sort of preliminary offer?'

'I can see you're way ahead of me, Dr Nielson,' Jill Cramer said, realising that there was more to the man than she had first supposed. She had taken him for a typical scientific type — soft-natured and with little head for hard business. She had been wrong. Nielson was a man who liked to be very much in control of a situation, and she guessed he could be quite ruthless when it came to getting exactly what he wanted.

'Of course, you realise that I'm not empowered to discuss actual salary and that sort of thing,' she resumed, eventually. 'Suffice it to say that Landsberg are more than willing to make you an extremely attractive proposition. If you're willing, we can drive down right now. I have an interview all lined up.'

Nielson smiled. 'I can't wait to experience that dangerous driving of yours. It's been some time since I had a little excitement in my life.'

Chapter Three

Annie Gilmour locked up her florist's shop door and walked down the street towards the bus depot. She passed a news vendor, hawking out the front-page screamer from the late afternoon edition of the *Evening Times*.

'Read all about it. More skulls found on the link road. More skulls on the link road. Read all about it.'

Annie stopped in her tracks, her face paling. Digging into her handbag for some small change, she practically snatched the newspaper out of the vendor's hand and strode away without waiting for her change.

She paused in a shop doorway to read the front page. There, grinning inanely, the truck driver proudly displayed his macabre find.

There was no humour in the picture for Annie. Grim-faced, she looked around for the nearest telephone box. Finding one vacant, she stepped in and dialled the number of Maryhill Police Station.

'Hello – can I speak to Detective Chief Inspector Jim Taggart, please? It's Mrs Gilmour – Annie Gilmour. He knows me.'

There was a pause on the other end of the line. Annie waited anxiously as the desk sergeant tried to locate Taggart.

Finally, she received an apologetic reply.

'Sorry, madam, but DCI Taggart doesn't seem to be in the building just now. I think he's out taking a tea-break at the moment.'

Annie sighed with disappointment. 'Well, could you please tell him that I called. And ask him to contact me just as soon as he can.' With a heavy heart, Annie hung up the receiver.

The desk sergeant was wrong. Taggart was not taking a tea-break. Instead, he was still very much on the job, in the distinctly unpleasant environment of the mortuary laboratory.

Dr Andrews placed the two skulls gently down on the shelf.

'Well, they're both female, for a start,' he announced. 'The fact that the sutures have not quite closed up at the top would suggest that they are both aged approximately between twenty-one and thirty.'

'Can you narrow that down?' Taggart asked.

Andrews gave him a questioning look. 'Got anyone in mind?'

'Aye. I could have.' He was obviously not willing, or not prepared, to volunteer any further information.

'Well, let's say mid to late twenties,' Andrews said, a little more specifically. 'Of course, I can't tell you how long they've been in the ground, or even if they were buried at the same time. Only the soil analysis will tell us that.'

'Any idea at this stage how they died?'

Dr Andrews gave a faint shrug. 'I can tell you how they didn't,' he said, helpfully. 'There are no injuries to the cranium. Only to the jaws — and those injuries were definitely inflicted after death. And probably after decapitation from the bodies.'

Taggart regarded the skulls moodily. He had been hoping for more initial information.

The mortuary door sighed open. Jardine came in, looking more hopeful. 'They've found hair strands in the soil around both skull sites. Both blonde.'

'Well, that's something,' Taggart muttered.

'Oh, by the way. There was a phone call for you, from Annie Gilmour,' Jardine added, remembering the message he had been given on his way out of the station.

Taggart chewed at his bottom lip. 'I thought there would be.'

Doctor Andrews suddenly understood their earlier conversation. 'She was blonde, wasn't she?'

Taggart nodded. 'And about twenty-four years old.'

He turned to Jardine. 'Well, I suppose we'd better go and report what we have so far to the chief.'

'Which isn't much,' Jardine observed.

Taggart shot him a withering look. 'Thanks for reminding me.'

Superintendent McVitie reviewed the brief case notes which Jardine had given him. There wasn't much to read. Scanning the few lines quickly, he looked up from his desk. 'So we're unlikely to learn much more until we get the report from the soil analysis lab?'

'That's about it, sir,' Taggart agreed. 'Of course, we've widened the search area. The rest of the bodies could have been buried nearby. It's more than likely.'

'This damage to the jawbones. Might that provide some sort of lead for us?' Jardine put in. 'After all, it's interesting that he did that as well as remove the teeth. Almost as though he knew something about forensic dentistry.'

Taggart chose to ignore the interruption, although he made a mental note to pursue the matter further. Jardine had a point, he admitted to himself ruefully. A point which he had missed. 'We're doing the usual missing person check,' he said to McVitie. 'One, of course, stands out.'

'Janet Gilmour,' McVitie said flatly, following Taggart's drift.

'The age is about right. Same colour of hair,' Taggart pointed out.

'Has her mother been in touch?'

Taggart nodded. 'Naturally, sir. I haven't spoken to her, but she left a message.'

McVitie pondered for a moment. 'Couldn't we superimpose the skull on a portrait of her? Like they did in the Ruxton case?' he suggested at length.

Jardine took a photograph of Janet Gilmour out of his file and pushed it along McVitie's desk. 'We're informed that wouldn't be successful in this case — for a number of reasons, sir. First of all, she has quite a full face in all the photos we have, and the way she wore her hair covered a great deal of her face anyway. I believe that in the Ruxton case, the victim had a thin, angular face with very high cheekbones.'

McVitie looked impressed with the young man's knowledge. 'Aren't you a little young to remember the Ruxton case?' he queried.

Jardine preened slightly at the implied praise. He opened his mouth to explain his interest in unusual and innovative forensic detective work, but Taggart cut him off.

'Oh, it was a classic of its kind, sir,' he said to McVitie, with a sideways glance at his young assistant and the trace of a smile on his face.

Jardine smiled ruefully. Taggart had done it again, managing to turn a moment of potential triumph into a put-down. One of these days he was going to learn!

'Well, I'd better go and see Annie Gilmour,' Taggart announced suddenly, bringing the discussion to a close.

Jardine looked sympathetic. He knew how depressing his superior found these encounters with bereaved parents. 'Would you like me to come with you, sir?'

Taggart shook his head heavily. 'No, it's best I go alone. It's become a personal thing, over the years.'

The faintest trace of concern registered on McVitie's face. 'Perhaps a bit *too* personal, Jim?'

Taggart sighed. 'Aye, perhaps.' Without another word, he left the room.

Annie Gilmour opened the door of her bungalow with a faint smile of greeting. She had seen Taggart arrive in his car through the window. She had been waiting for him, knowing that he would come, sooner or later.

'Hello, Jim. It's good of you to come,' she said softly.

Taggart returned the forced smile. 'I'm sorry I couldn't contact you earlier, but it's been a busy day.'

'You must think me a terrible nuisance — ringing you every time like this,' Annie said, apologetically.

Taggart moved past her into the lounge. He seated himself in an armchair without waiting for an invitation. There was no need. He had been to this house many times over the past four years. He waited until Annie had seated herself opposite him.

'Annie, Annie,' he said gently. 'Surely you've learned by now that there's no need to apologise. I understand. I've always understood.'

Annie nodded. She had come to trust Jim Taggart as a friend, and not as a policeman. But there was always the need for that little ritual, that token apology and token dismissal between them.

'It's just that . . . as soon as I read the papers . . . I had to know,' she said.

Taggart spread his hands in an almost hopeless gesture.

'The plain truth of the situation is that we just don't know much at all at the moment,' he said, bluntly but not unkindly.

'They said that two skulls were found. Is there a possibility . . .?' Annie asked. 'I mean — are they female? Can you tell that much?'

Taggart chose his words very carefully. 'Look, Annie — I don't want to build up your hopes, like last time . . .'

Annie cut him short. 'Just if there's a possibility, Jim. That's all I'm asking. That's all I want to know.'

Taggart hesitated for several seconds, his face impassive. Finally, he nodded. 'Yes, there's a possibility,' he admitted. 'Both skulls are female, both were blondes and both probably around Janet's age. But that's about the strength of it at the moment.'

The merest hint of hope seemed to wipe years of strain from the woman's face. She smiled, almost happily. 'You know, it's almost four years to the day, Jim. Next Friday. It would be strange, wouldn't it, if she was found almost four years to the day?'

'We probably won't know that quickly,' Taggart pointed out, feeling a strong need to do so.

Annie accepted it philosophically. 'I've been patient for four years, Jim. I can wait a few more days. Look, would you like a drink? Some supper, perhaps?'

Taggart pushed himself to his feet somewhat reluctantly. He understood the woman's need for company, but he had his own life to lead, and his own problems. Although his wife and he were little more than two strangers occupying the same house these days, he still owed her at least some of his time.

'No, thank you, Annie, I'd best be getting home. Jean will have put supper on the table for me,' he lied, knowing that she had long since given up preparing food which would probably be wasted.

He moved towards the door.

'I promise I'll keep you informed,' he said gently.

'One way or the other?' Annie prompted.

'Aye. One way . . . or the other.' Taggart let himself out and walked towards his car without a backward glance.

Annie waited until he had driven out of sight before closing her front door. She walked, slowly, into one of the bedrooms. It was a young girl's room, but more than that, it was a shrine.

A dress still hung on the back of the door, looking as though it had just been taken off. Other clothes lay neatly folded on a bedside chair, waiting for their owner to slip into them. On the bed, a large teddy bear lay on the pillow, waiting to be taken between the sheets and cuddled.

Annie moved to the dressing-table, still laid out neatly with all the grooming tools and make-up requirements of a young and beautiful girl.

The beautiful, blonde-haired girl in the framed photograph took pride of place on top of the vanity unit.

Annie picked it up, gazing at the image of her lost daughter.

'Soon, my darling. Perhaps soon,' she murmured, a fond smile playing at her lips.

Annie touched her fingers to the photograph, tracing the line of the two gold amulets which hung around the girl's neck. They were a pair — one a glowing sun, the other a crescent moon. Replacing the photograph, Annie slid open one of the drawers and drew out a thin gold chain.

The shining golden sun dangled at the end of it. The moon was missing.

Janet had been wearing it on the night she disappeared.

Chapter Four

Jardine turned in to the City Arms and headed for the bar, nodding at several colleagues along the way. The place had become more or less the unofficial social club for Maryhill Police Station over the past couple of months.

Dr Andrews sidled up to him as he prepared to order his drink.

'How would you like to impress your superiors?' he asked with a knowing grin. Andrews was well aware of the ongoing duel between the young DS and Taggart, and right now he was in a position to turn it to his advantage. He drained his whisky glass and set it down on the counter under Jardine's nose. 'Large whisky, please.'

Jardine smiled ruefully and dug in his pocket.

'Well?' he asked eventually, when they had both been served.

'There's an old university chum of mine. Professor Peter Hutton. Widely acknowledged as one of the greatest experts in the technique of reconstructing faces on skulls. He's scored some amazing successes, I understand.'

Jardine nodded. 'Yes, I've heard of the technique. Based on the relationship between the face and the contours of the skull, I believe. But I thought most of that sort of work had been carried out in America?'

'Ah — that's where the good bit comes in,' Andrews said, tapping the side of his nose. 'He's right here in Glasgow at the moment. Oddly enough they brought him over to put faces to those two Roman skulls.'

Jardine was hooked. 'Where could I find him?'

Andrews drained his glass again and waited for Jardine to pay for another refill before continuing. 'Department of Anatomy at Glasgow University. You should be able to catch him in the morning.'

Jardine was feeling pleased with himself as he crossed the university campus on his way to the Department of Anatomy. It felt good to be one jump ahead of Taggart for a change.

There were two men in the room as he entered. One of them, scruffily dressed and in his middle fifties, was puffing at a cigarette with the nervous compulsion of the confirmed chain-smoker. An unprepossessing figure, he hardly looked the type to be a leading expert at anything.

Jardine addressed himself to the younger, smarter man.

'Excuse me, but I was looking for Professor Peter Hutton. Any idea where I might find him?'

Surprisingly, it was the older man who answered, somewhat brusquely. 'I'm Hutton. What do you want? I'm due at a press conference.'

Jardine produced his ID card. 'Detective Sergeant Michael Jardine, Maryhill Station. I need a few words. It should only take a couple of minutes.'

Hutton turned to his companion. 'Carl, could you go ahead to the lecture room and tell them I'm on my way?'

As Carl Young left the room, Hutton lit another cigarette from the burning stub between his fingers and regarded Jardine over a cloud of blue smoke.

'What's all this about?'

'An old colleague of yours, Dr Stephen Andrews, said you might be able to help us,' Jardine told him.

'Ah, Stephen,' Hutton mused. 'Has he still got that ridiculous beard?' Without waiting for an answer, he made a move towards the door. 'Look, can we discuss this on the way to the lecture hall? I'm running late as it is.'

Jardine followed the man back outside. There were several people loitering and strolling around the campus. Jardine failed to spot Mike Gallagher, a reporter from the *Evening Times* who had tailed him all the way from Maryhill Station. Gallagher fell into step slightly behind them, his ears pricked.

'There would have to be a fee, of course,' Hutton said when Jardine had explained the position. 'For the department, of course — you understand?'

'I can't authorise that off my own back,' Jardine told him. 'But I'm sure something can be arranged.'

It seemed to satisfy Hutton. 'How much do you know about my work?'

Jardine shrugged. 'Very little,' he admitted. 'The point is, do you think you can help us?'

'Oh, I should think so.' Hutton sounded very confident. 'I did a similar job for the police in Chicago not so long ago. They had three skulls in a trunk and no bodies. I put faces on all three, and they positively identified two of them. What do you know about yours so far?'

'Only that they are both young females. That's about it.'

'Hair samples?'

'Blonde, in both cases.'

Hutton seemed to be weighing things up in his mind. 'Well, it sounds like I should be able to help you. Dependent on the fee, of course. The Americans are most generous in these matters, I seem to recall.'

They had reached the entrance to the lecture hall.

'Look — this is not official yet, so I'd be obliged if you didn't say anything,' Jardine said.

Hutton didn't seem to be listening any more. He strode up the steps of the lecture hall, pausing only to light up yet another cigarette. He was closely followed by Gallagher.

Jardine walked back to his car, congratulating himself on a good morning's work. There was the problem of the fee, of course, but he was certain Taggart could make sure that some funds were made available.

Inside the lecture hall, Hutton took his place on the rostrum. Carl Young had laid out everything neatly for him in readiness: his notes, and plaster casts of the two Roman skulls.

Hutton picked one of them up and addressed his small audience, launching into his prepared speech. 'Good morning, ladies and gentlemen. I'd like you to meet Flavius Hierombalus and his auxiliary here. I invented Flavius because it was a common first name at the time.'

Gallagher climbed to his feet, interrupting Hutton in full flow. 'Professor Hutton — can you tell us any more about the work you are doing on the two murder victims' skulls found yesterday?'

Hutton was completely thrown off guard. 'I haven't started yet.'

'But you have helped police forces before with this sort of thing?'

'Well, yes,' Hutton admitted.

Gallagher smiled with satisfaction, having obtained an official confirmation. 'And you will be able to reconstruct their faces just as you could on these Roman ones?' he prompted.

'Yes, the principle is exactly the same,' Hutton agreed.

Gallagher sat down again, more than pleased with himself.

The story made the midday edition. It also made Taggart's office. Scowling furiously, Taggart waved the newspaper under Jardine's nose.

'What are you — a one-man band?' he demanded angrily.

Jardine cowered slightly under the attack. 'I told him not to say anything,' he muttered defensively. 'I thought I was using my initiative.'

Taggart took a few seconds off to read the newspaper story fully, calming down as he realised that his young colleague had, actually, made a significant breakthrough. 'I've got nothing against you using your initiative,' he said finally, in a less aggressive tone. 'Just as long as you keep me informed.' Taggart pointed to the photograph of Hutton. 'What is this guy? Some kind of witch-doctor?'

Jardine relaxed, knowing that Taggart's anger had dissipated. 'Why don't we go and find out?' he suggested.

Taggart's suspicions of witch-doctory were confirmed by his first sight of Hutton's work lab. Rows of human skulls and various pieces of bone littered the shelves and work-tops. A human skeleton in one corner of the room had been pressed into service as a coat rack and the man had even found a use for one piece of skull as an ashtray, into which he ritually tapped the ash from his ubiquitous cigarette.

Jardine placed the large cardboard box he had been carrying upon the nearest work-top. Opening it, he gently lifted out the two skulls.

Hutton weighed them both in his hands as though he were testing two melons for ripeness. 'And one of these you believe to be the skull of Janet Gilmour?' he asked.

Taggart nodded. 'That's right. We're going on estimated age alone — so we figure skull number two. They're both tabbed.'

Hutton selected the correct skull and examined it carefully. 'The teeth and jawbone might be a bit of a problem, but I can probably build it up reasonably accurately. Have you brought the hair samples?'

Jardine produced two plastic bags, also tagged and numbered. 'Do you need a photograph of Janet?'

Hutton shook his head. 'I don't want to know what she looked like. It might affect my reconstruction. I'm a scientist, not a sculptor.'

'How long will it take?' Taggart wanted to know.

Hutton considered for a moment. 'Well, I should do a bit more work on the Roman skulls. There's an exhibition next week.'

'They'll have to wait,' Taggart snapped testily. He was still slightly miffed about the size of Hutton's fee. 'They've been around for two thousand years. I'm sure they'll wait a bit longer.'

Hutton shrugged carelessly. 'I'll start on them as soon as I can. I'll be in touch when I have something to show you.'

He was obviously unwilling to be more specific. Taggart decided that he wasn't going to achieve much by pressing the man. Besides, the ghoulish lab unnerved him slightly, and he couldn't wait to be out of it. 'Right, then — we'll leave you to it,' he muttered, turning to leave.

Jardine followed him rather reluctantly. He had found the place totally fascinating.

Chapter Five

Taggart came down for breakfast to find Jean seated in her wheelchair cuddling a large ginger cat. He groaned aloud. 'Aw, Jean — you know I can't stand cats.'

His wife was instantly on the defensive. 'He'll keep me company during the day. And most of the evenings, seeing as you're hardly ever here.'

Taggart accepted the implied rebuke without comment. 'Where did it come from, anyway?'

'Mrs MacPherson asked me to have it. They're moving to a new flat and they're not allowed to keep pets.'

'Did she not have a dog?' Taggart asked. 'At least you can talk to a dog.'

'And who would walk it?' Jean countered. 'You'd never find the time.'

Taggart could sense that his wife was warming to her old, familiar theme. He decided to skip breakfast. Putting on his tie, he prepared to leave.

'You will make an effort to be home for our Burns Supper on Friday?' Jean queried. 'You'll remember I mentioned it to you last week. I've invited Margaret MacKenzie and her family, and we're having a disabled piper.'

Taggart groaned again. He had vague memories about the supper, but the disabled piper was something new. 'You're not seriously having bagpipes in this house?' he said, as though it had been some kind of a joke.

'And why not?' Jean demanded. She had thought it was a rather good idea.

Her husband managed a faint smile. 'Well, all I can say is, he really will be disabled if the neighbours come round.'

The telephone started to ring. Taggart moved to answer it.

'You will try to get home in time, won't you?' Jean stressed, anxious to pin him down to some sort of commitment before his mind was taken up with other things.

'You know me, Jean. I always try,' Taggart answered, picking up the phone.

It was Mike Jardine. He sounded depressed. 'Sir — Hutton's lab was broken into last night. Someone stole the skulls.'

'What!' Taggart shouted, hardly able to believe his ears. 'Was there no damned security there at all?'

'I doubt if it would have made much difference, sir,' Jardine told him. 'The thief was pretty determined. He smashed open two doors and forced the outside lock as it was.'

'Meet me there in ten minutes,' Taggart snapped. He tugged his tie into position and reached for his coat. He left without remembering to say goodbye to his wife.

Although, as Jardine had explained, there was a lot of external damage caused by the break-in, there was virtually no disruption to the lab itself. To Taggart, it was patently obvious that the thief had known exactly what he was looking for.

Hutton was distraught. 'They're utterly irreplaceable. Priceless,' he complained bitterly, sucking at his cigarette angrily.

Taggart did a double-take. 'Wait a minute. Priceless, did you say? What skulls are we talking about here?'

Hutton looked at him as though he were a simpleton. 'Why, the Roman skulls of course. Why do you think I'm so upset?'

'You mean — *our* skulls weren't taken?' Taggart asked, hardly able to believe his luck.

'Of course they didn't take *your* skulls,' Hutton said peevishly. 'They're quite safe in the bottom of the cupboard over there.' He indicated a wall cupboard across the room.

Jardine beat Taggart to the cupboard by a clear couple of feet. Reaching in, he drew out a small, plain cardboard box and carried it back over to the work-top.

'Now let's get this clear,' Taggart said, trying to make sense of the whole business. 'How many skulls are we actually talking about?'

'Two, of course,' Hutton said. 'They've stolen the two Roman skulls and all the plaster casts I had made of them.'

'And none of the skulls are ours?' Taggart double-checked.

'Only the plaster casts, apparently,' Jardine put in. 'But they can always be made again.' He stared closely at the box he had just carried from the cupboard. 'Wait a minute — this isn't the box I brought the skulls in. Ours had "Strathclyde Police" clearly stamped on it. This one is completely plain.'

Hutton regarded him as though he was mad. 'Someone has stolen two of the most important archaeological finds in years — and you're worried about a *box*?' he said, as though he couldn't quite believe it.

But Jardine wasn't really listening. 'Our box — where is it?' he demanded.

Hutton glowered at him. 'How the devil should I know? I'm a professor of anatomy, not cardboard boxes.'

Taggart, who had only just realised the full significance of what Jardine was saying, jumped to his colleague's assistance. He turned on Hutton angrily. 'This is your lab, and you're responsible for the things in it. That box was entrusted to your care. Now where is it?'

Hutton's incredulity turned to fury. The whole business of the box seemed like the worst possible case of petty bureaucracy bordering on the obsessional. 'I am not responsible for the security of this university. Nor do I spend my nights with my work.'

The lab door opened at that moment, and Carl Young walked in. He looked surprised at the unusual activity. 'What's going on?'

'Someone broke in last night. They've stolen the two Hamian skulls and all the plaster casts we made of them. It's all gone — everything — and all the damned police seem to be worried about is a blasted cardboard box.'

'We've every right to be,' Jardine pointed out, pointing to the plain box on the work-top. 'That is not the box we brought our skulls in.'

Carl Young stepped over to the cupboard and peered inside. Returning, he too looked at the box on the lab table. 'I cleared up last night. I must have put the skulls back into different boxes. Why, does it matter much?'

'Of course it matters,' Taggart said, explaining as if to a child. 'It means that whoever stole those skulls thought he was stealing ours. He wasn't after your Roman skulls at all.' He turned back to Hutton. 'I'll have to have this lab closed off for a few hours,' he informed the man. 'In the meantime, I don't want anything touched until the fingerprint boys have finished their work. Is that clear?'

Hutton nodded wordlessly.

'Right — everybody out,' Taggart said, ushering them all towards the door.

Outside, in the university grounds, Taggart chose a position from which he could view the Department of Anatomy building as a whole.

'I want twenty-four-hour security on this place from now on,' he told Jardine. 'They might as well have put out welcome notices for the thief. Hutton's name was on the door and there are no checks at all on who goes in or out of the building. All our man had to do was to hide somewhere inside until everyone had gone home for the night.'

'Is it our murderer, do you think, sir? Or just some sort of ghoul?' Jardine mused.

'A ghoul would have found plenty in there without ransacking cupboards,' Taggart observed. He paused, thoughtfully. 'On the other hand — why would our murderer fear his victim being identified?'

Jardine followed the line of reasoning to its logical conclusion. 'Unless he was directly connected to them in some way,' he finished off.

Taggart nodded. 'Right.'

Jardine's face clouded over. 'The trouble is, sir — that puts us up another blind alley. You checked out all Janet Gilmour's possible contacts — friends, work colleagues, enemies — when you were investigating her disappearance.'

Taggart dismissed the objection. 'We're not even sure that one of the victims is Janet Gilmour yet,' he reminded his colleague. 'And if it is, perhaps she might have been connected to the killer only *indirectly* — through the second victim.'

'It's rather a long shot,' Jardine pointed out.

'Aye,' Taggart sighed. 'But at the moment it's the only one we've got.'

Chapter Six

Dr Nielson stepped through the glass entrance doors of Casco Pharmaceuticals and headed across the lobby towards the security desk to pick up his pass. From the corner of his eye he saw Maureen MacDonald, the company's research director, heading in his direction and muttered a silent curse. He had been hoping to avoid the woman — at least for the day. She was almost certain to want to pry into the reason for his absence the previous afternoon, and Nielson wanted things to be kept as discreet as possible until he had had a chance to talk to Casco's managing director, Derek Amlot.

However, he managed a polite smile, much as he personally disliked the woman. Nielson had no real objection to a female research director, unlike some of his male colleagues. What he did object to was the way in which she had risen to her position — by riding on the research successes of other scientists and by substituting a talent for administration for genuine hands-on scientific work.

'Ah, just the man,' Maureen gushed. 'Dr Nielson, you do remember that there is the quarterly work study with the accountancy team this afternoon? And Derek arrives back from his Far East trip at around five-thirty and will probably want a report update.'

'I go home at five-thirty,' Nielson said firmly.

The intended rebuff backfired, giving Maureen MacDonald the perfect opportunity to bring up the one topic which Nielson had wanted to avoid. 'You left early yesterday,' she pointed out, leaving a slight inflection at the end of the statement which begged an explanatory response.

'Yes, I went to the School of Tropical Medicine in Liverpool,' Nielson lied, off the top of his head. 'I was hoping to obtain an Australian taipan. That's a venomous snake which grows to a length of twelve feet.'

Maureen gave a little shudder. 'I hope I never meet one of those.'

'It probably wouldn't be too happy to meet you, either,' Nielson muttered unkindly. Picking up his pass from the desk, he walked away towards his lab.

The corridor was blocked by Dennis and his tea-trolley, with a small queue of people waiting to be served. Rather than attempt to push past, Nielson waited patiently in line, returning the warm smile which Dennis flashed at him. The young man was willing, and always smiling, albeit a trifle vacantly. Mentally retarded, with the approximate intellect of a twelve-year-old, Dennis had become a familiar sight throughout the building over the past five years, forever trundling his trolley up and down the corridors and dispensing drinks and snacks. Nielson always tried to be friendly to him, unlike some other staff members who treated the unfortunate young man with disdain.

Angus Mackay, who was in the queue immediately ahead of Nielson, was a prime offender in this respect. He grimaced as he sipped the cup of tea which Dennis had just handed to him. 'What's in this tea, boy?' he demanded gruffly. 'It tastes foul.'

Dennis looked hurt. 'Just the usual, Dr Mackay.'

Mackay turned on Nielson. 'My God, I think I shall need one of your anti-venoms after drinking this filth.'

Nielson said nothing. He disliked Mackay, with his grandilo-
quent air and his foppish way of wearing bow-ties with his lab coat.
However, he had to respect the man as a scientist. Specialising in
allergies, he was an acknowledged leader in his field.

'I suppose Maureen nabbed you on your way in,' Mackay went
on to Nielson. 'Another bloody pow-wow with the accountants.
Wouldn't it be nice if we could all get on with the job of being
scientists? That bloody woman wouldn't know sodium chloride if
she ate it.'

Nielson grunted, feeling some sort of response was called for
but not wishing to be drawn into one of Mackay's frequent
moaning sessions.

Deprived of an ally, Mackay vented his spleen on the unfortunate Dennis. 'I shall make it my business to see that you are
replaced by a vending machine, boy,' he said nastily, slamming his
cup of tea back on the trolley and storming off.

Dennis stared after him, his normally smiling face seething with
a mixture of hate and fear.

Nielson picked up his own cup and headed for his lab. Reaching
it, he stepped inside and closed the door behind him most
gratefully.

Christine Gray looked up from her microscope. 'Good morning, Dr Nielson. I hope you're feeling better.'

Nielson suddenly remembered that he had made the excuse
about feeling unwell the previous day. And he had just spun
Maureen MacDonald the story about the Australian taipan. He
felt slightly guilty. Christine had always been a devoted and totally
efficient assistant. Nielson felt she deserved the truth. 'Look, this
is in the strictest confidence, Christine — but I actually went for
an interview yesterday. Landsberg Chemicals in Liverpool. They
want me to head up a new research project.'

The faintest look of disappointment crossed Christine's face,
but she controlled it. 'And have you accepted?'

'I said I'd give them my answer tomorrow,' Nielson said. 'I have
to speak to Derek Amlot first, it's only good form.'

'He won't be very happy,' Christine observed, only too well

aware of the potential cash value of Nielson's current research. 'What do you think he'll do?'

'Oh, he'll top Landsberg's offer, that's certain,' Nielson said confidently.

'And would you stay then?'

Nielson shook his head slowly. 'It's not just the money, Christine. It's the whole system in this place. No, Derek Amlot is in for an unpleasant surprise, I'm afraid.'

'And your wife? How does she feel about it?' Christine asked.

Nielson suddenly seemed less confident. 'She'll just have to accept it,' he answered, his face clouding over as he thought of the inevitable confrontation.

In fact, it looked like being less of a confrontation than a fleeting skirmish. Morag Nielson was obviously preparing to go out when her husband entered the house.

Nielson watched her make the final adjustments to her hair and make-up in the hall mirror with a slight sinking feeling in his stomach. At thirty-five, a full ten years younger than her husband, Morag was still a strikingly attractive woman. Although they continued to share the same bed, and occasionally made love, Nielson had no doubts that she had affairs with other men, and the knowledge stung. He had never really had too many illusions about their marriage. He had been attracted to Morag purely by her looks, and she had seen the financial potential of a young scientist with a good brain and even better prospects. The marriage had not, perhaps, been made in heaven — but it had certainly turned out to be made on the right side of town. Their luxurious home, in a fashionable suburb of the city, was the envy of their friends. In the past three years, their lifestyle had been even further improved by Morag's own business as a freelance business consultant — her personal income now fast approaching that of her husband.

'Where are you off to?' Nielson asked.

Morag frowned slightly, as though she resented the question.

'Just meeting a new client. He has his own catering business but hasn't kept any books for three years. Should be fun.'

'I suppose you're having dinner with him?'

Morag flashed him a pitying look. 'Well, we're not going to sit on a street corner. Why, does it matter?'

'I wanted to talk to you,' Nielson said.

Morag grimaced. 'God, that sounds ominous.'

'The thing is, I went to Liverpool yesterday. I had an interview with Landsberg Chemicals, Casco's biggest rivals. They've offered me a job. Ten thousand a year more than I'm getting now, and increased research facilities.'

'Only ten? I thought you'd have been worth more than that,' Morag muttered dismissively.

'I need to talk it over with you,' Nielson went on, ignoring the put-down. 'It's important.'

'Not to me, it isn't,' Morag said bluntly.

'It would mean selling up, moving down to Liverpool to live. It would be a major change in our lives,' Nielson pointed out.

Morag turned away from admiring herself in the mirror to face him directly for the first time. Her face was set and impassive. 'There's no question of moving to Liverpool,' she said flatly. 'I have clients here in Glasgow. I can't just give them up.'

'You could get new clients in Liverpool.'

Morag adopted a patronising tone, as though addressing a small child. 'I don't want to get new clients. I don't want to go to Liverpool. I don't want my life disrupted. I like it here. Why should I give up what I've got just so that you can earn another ten thousand a year that we don't need?'

'It's not just the money,' Nielson said for the second time in the day.

'What, then?' Morag demanded. 'You've never complained about research facilities before.' Her eyes narrowed with suspicion. 'Why this sudden desire to get out of Glasgow, anyway?'

Nielson shrugged, feeling beaten. 'You wouldn't understand.'

Morag returned her attention to the mirror, making a final adjustment to her hair. 'Anyway, I haven't time to talk about this now. I'm late as it is. You will throw these things at me. Anyway — if it's that important to you, you could always take a flat down there during the week and come home whenever you had some free time.'

Nielson looked shocked. 'You don't think I'd leave you alone up here, do you?'

'No, of course not,' Morag said, with a trace of bitterness. She looked disappointed. For a moment she thought she had come up with the answer to several of her personal problems at once. 'Anyway, I have to go.' Morag moved towards the door.

'Morag — I can't make this decision on my own,' Nielson pleaded after her.

She turned, regarding him with that now familiar look of pity and condescension. 'Douglas, you've managed to make decisions in your life before without consulting me. I should have thought that this one was obvious.'

On this ambiguous note she left, closing the door behind her.

Nielson stared at the door stupidly for a few seconds, his face twitching slightly with a mixture of conflicting emotions. He hated the woman, he realised — but he was damned if he was going to let her get away from him that easily. Besides his work, Nielson had virtually nothing of which he could proudly boast — 'this is mine'.

And Morag was his . . . and Nielson intended to make sure things stayed that way.

Chapter Seven

The Link Road excavation site looked even more of a moonscape under the harsh white glare of arc lights.

Taggart, Jardine and DC Jackie Reid trudged through the mud towards a cordoned-off area where Dr Andrews was waiting for them. He stood above one of the many shallow pits which had been excavated by police workmen all over the site.

Reaching it, Taggart looked down into the four-feet-deep hole. The bones of a headless skeleton seemed to glow eerily in the glare of the lights.

'Does it belong to one of the heads?' Taggart asked.

Andrews stopped. 'Too early to say for sure – but it's more than likely.' He nodded across the site towards another excavation, also brightly lit. 'The other one's over there.'

'Have fun with the jigsaw puzzle,' Taggart told him, striding off to view the second skeleton.

Outside the police cordon a car pulled up and a woman climbed out. Recognising her, Taggart touched Jackie Reid on the arm. 'See that woman over there? Go and tell her to go away. I don't want her here. She's Janet Gilmour's mother.'

Jackie Reid nodded, setting off at a tangent to intercept Annie Gilmour as she made her way towards the first row of police tapes.

Taggart and Jardine reached the edge of the second, slightly shallower, pit and peered down. Another decapitated skeleton was there, laid out in exactly the same strange way that the first one had been.

'Peculiar, that positioning of the arms,' Jardine observed.

Taggart nodded. 'Arms crossed over the chest, in both cases. A strange beastie, our murderer. He hacks the heads off his victims, yet he poses their skeletons as though they were laid out for a religious burial. Suggest anything to you?'

'A religious nut, sir?' Jardine suggested. 'Some sort of obsessional psychopath, at least.'

Taggart turned away from the pit. 'Well, there's not much we can do here until they move these skeletons to the mortuary lab. What say we go and see if our witch-doctor friend keeps nocturnal hours?'

Jackie Reid led Annie Gilmour across to meet them as they returned to their car. She had given the woman a mug of hot tea from the police refreshment wagon, which Annie clutched tightly between tensed, quivering fingers. 'She wouldn't go, sir — not until she had spoken to you.'

Taggart nodded understandingly. He put his arm around Annie's shoulder and led her to his car. 'You shouldn't be here, Annie,' he reproved her gently.

Annie's voice quavered slightly. 'I know, Jim. But I had to come — just to see for myself.'

Taggart hugged her. 'Oh, Annie. I know how hard it has been — but now that we might be getting close, you have to back off a little.'

Jackie Reid nudged Jardine in the ribs, nodding across at Taggart and Annie. 'Is the chief a bit soft on her or something?'

Jardine shook his head. 'He's kept in touch with her ever since her daughter disappeared. Then her husband died, and there was nothing . . . for years.'

Taggart seated Annie in the car, closed the door and then stepped round to let himself in beside her. Annie sipped at her tea for a few seconds, staring out through the windscreen towards the glare of the arc lights.

'That young police girl wouldn't tell me anything,' she muttered finally, in a strangely detached tone. 'But I could see that you've found something.'

'You still shouldn't have come,' Taggart told her.

Annie continued to stare blankly out through the windscreen. 'Jim, I've spent four years sitting at home wondering . . . waiting. I just can't sit at home any more. Ken died doing just that. I know she's dead — I just want to know where she is and how she died.'

'Annie, she may not be dead,' Taggart reminded her. It had always been a possibility.

Annie shook her head sadly. 'No, Jim. You don't believe that, and neither do I. If Janet was alive, she would have found some way to contact me.'

'Part of me wants to believe it,' Taggart said. 'And part of me wants you to know one way or the other.'

'Well, what have you found?' Annie asked, suddenly becoming totally matter-of-fact.

Taggart hesitated before answering. He wasn't sure whether to tell her or not. Finally, he decided that there was no real reason why she should not know. 'There are two skeletons,' he said simply.

'And clothes . . . what about clothes?'

Taggart averted his eyes. 'There is no evidence of clothes,' he muttered awkwardly, knowing the implications of that statement.

Annie sighed, as though confirming something that she had always known. 'Can I just go and take a look?' she pleaded.

Taggart put his foot down. 'Annie, there is no way I'm going to let you walk out there,' he said firmly. 'You'll just have to leave it with us for a while longer. We can tell things from skeletons — measure the height, check medical records. And we already have a guy putting faces on the two skulls.'

'I know about that,' Annie said. 'I read it in the papers.'

'Then you'll realise that we may not be too far away from a

positive identification,' Taggart said, his tone softening again. 'Trust me, Annie. You know I'll tell you just the second we know for sure.'

Annie smiled faintly. 'Of course I trust you, Jim. I've always trusted you.'

Taggart took her hand and squeezed it. 'Come on, let's see about getting you home. I've got to go and see how our expert is getting on with the facial reconstruction.'

They climbed out of the car. Taggart beckoned Jackie Reid over. 'See Mrs Gilmour to her car. Perhaps you could take her home. Dr Andrews can supervise the transfer of the skeletons to the lab.'

'Yes, sir.' Jackie took Annie gently by the arm and started to lead her away.

Taggart watched her walk away, seeing the reluctance in her step. He shook his head, sadly, then turned away and headed for Jardine.

Jardine spoke to the young constable on duty outside the university buildings.

'Anybody still here?'

'Professor Hutton left a couple of hours ago, sir. His assistant is still working, I believe.'

Taggart clicked his teeth with annoyance. 'That man doesn't seem to have any sense of urgency,' he complained. 'Well, let's go and see if his assistant has anything new for us.'

Jardine followed him into the building and up the stairs towards the Department of Anatomy.

Carl Young was hard at work as they entered. On the work-top in front of him a fresh cast of one of the skulls had already been built up with a new jaw and a set of teeth. Picking up a fine electric drill, Young drilled a couple of small holes just above the eye sockets, which had been filled with two plastic bubbles.

Seeing Taggart and Jardine, he laid the drill down and looked up at them. 'I didn't expect you back quite so soon. Is there anything I can do for you?'

'Where's Hutton?' Taggart wanted to know.

'Still trying to placate the archaeologists over the stolen skulls, I should think,' Young answered. 'They're pretty upset about it all.'

Jardine nodded to the skull on the work-top. 'Is that the new cast?'

Young nodded. 'Peter had to recreate the missing pieces of jawbone from moulding compound. The teeth are real — they belonged to a girl of approximately the same age.'

'And he just happened to have them lying around?' Taggart said, with heavy sarcasm.

Young slid open a drawer, displaying its contents. Lined up in rows of graded sizes were at least thirty sets of human teeth.

Taggart grimaced. 'Sorry I asked.'

'I noticed you drilling holes into the skull,' Jardine observed. 'What were they for?'

'Just strategic points where we insert cocktail sticks to the thickness of the soft tissue. Before putting the clay on and sculpting actual features,' Young informed him.

'Look, no disrespect intended, but I thought Professor Hutton was supposed to be doing this work,' Taggart said.

Young smiled. 'Oh, this is merely the groundwork. Done to fairly basic calculations. Peter takes over when it comes to the sculpting. I've watched him do it many times. He's quite a genius.'

The telephone rang. Young rose to answer it, then held out the receiver and called over to Taggart.

'It's for you. A Dr Andrews.'

'I'll answer it, sir,' Jardine offered. There was no objection from his superior, so he crossed the room and took the phone from Young's hand.

Young returned to his work bench.

'You're very attached to Professor Hutton, aren't you?' Taggart asked him.

Young looked up, his eyes slightly shifty. 'I respect his work, certainly.'

'But no more than that?'

Young looked embarrassed. 'I'm not sure I know what you mean.'

47

Taggart gave him a knowing smile. 'Oh, I'm sure you do,' he murmured.

Jardine replaced the telephone and returned. 'That was the preliminary report of the two skeletons. They do fit the skulls. One of them would have an overall living stature of between five foot five and six inches — the other between five foot four and five.'

'Janet Gilmour was five foot five,' Taggart muttered.

'So are a lot of females, sir,' Jardine pointed out.

'Aye,' Taggart agreed with a sigh. 'But until we can be sure, Annie Gilmour just waits and hopes.'

'Hopes that it isn't?' Jardine said.

Taggart shook his head. 'No — hopes that it is,' he corrected. 'She wants an end to all the wondering — and I can't say that I blame her.'

Jardine noted the troubled look on his superior's craggy face. 'I know it's not my place, sir,' he said sympathetically. 'But, well — you've become pretty personally involved with her over the years . . .'

Taggart didn't let him finish. 'You're right,' he snapped. 'It's not your place.'

Chapter Eight

Derek Amlot concealed quite a lot under his boyish good looks and amiable smile. He had not risen to be head of Casco Pharmaceuticals without considerable business acumen, and the company would not have prospered as it had done under his managing directorship unless he was quite ruthless in business matters.

His trip to Japan had tested both these abilities to the full. It had taken three days of hard negotiation, but Amlot had just clinched a deal which could, conceivably, write the company an open cheque in the coming years in the expanding and lucrative Far East market. A fair proportion of the potential business hinged on the current research work being conducted by Dr Nielson and his assistant, Christine Gray.

Maureen MacDonald was waiting for him as he strolled into his office, still feeling the effects of the long flight the previous afternoon.

'Good flight?' she enquired brightly.

Amlot grunted. 'The worst part was the connection at Heathrow. As usual. Any problems while I was away?'

Maureen shook her head. 'None that I know of. I've left all the new reports with Caroline. So when you're ready . . .'

Amlot reached for his office intercom and thumbed the button. 'No time like the present.' He waited a fraction of a second before his personal secretary answered. 'Oh, Caroline — could you come in, please. And bring the reports that Maureen left with you.'

'Oh, by the way,' Maureen said, suddenly remembering. 'Dr Nielson wants to see you some time today. He says it's very urgent.'

Amlot frowned. 'Tell him it's impossible. You see him, find out what he wants.'

'He insists on seeing you personally,' Maureen informed him. 'Obviously, if I could have handled it, I would have.'

Amlot was about to make a further comment when Caroline stepped briskly into the office. She dropped a sheaf of papers on to his desk. 'I've pencilled in a lunch with Sir Reginald Naughton at twelve-thirty. And you had an urgent telephone call from a woman. She wouldn't give her name. Her number is in your personal diary.'

'Thanks, Caroline.' Amlot looked up at Maureen. 'Could you give me a few minutes?'

'Of course.' Maureen followed Caroline out of the room into the outer office.

'Three guesses as to what that telephone number was?' Caroline whispered as she closed the office door behind her. She winked at Maureen in conspiratorial fashion.

'Mrs Nielson,' Maureen said. It was no secret around the office that Amlot had been having an affair with Nielson's wife for several months.

Caroline nodded, giggling. 'They're starting to get careless.'

'I don't want to lose you, Douglas,' Amlot said, after Nielson had explained his position. 'And especially not to Landsberg. I'm prepared to top any offer they've made you, you must realise that.'

'The money's not important, Derek. I'm simply not happy here.'

'Look, I know how you feel,' Amlot said in a conciliatory tone.

'Do you?' Nielson snapped back, not prepared to be sweet-talked out of his decision. 'I've given fifteen years of my life to Casco — and what have I got to show for it? That Natalvin business, for a start.'

Amlot spread his hands in a placatory gesture. 'Douglas, that was over four years ago. It was a mistake on my part at the time, and I'm sorry for it. But there's no need to bring it all up again now.'

Nielson would not be side-tracked. It was an old wound, and he had opened it up. Now it needed to be cauterised, once and for all. 'That was my research, my success. And Dr MacDonald's name went on the paper. This company has taken credit for everything I've done.'

Amlot sighed. 'I'm sorry you still feel bitter about that, Douglas. I really am. But we can make it up to you, if only you're prepared to stay — at least until you finish your current project. Then, perhaps in a year or two's time, you can think again.'

Nielson shook his head. 'No, I want to leave, Derek — and I want to leave now. I've made my decision.'

Amlot tried another tack. 'What does your wife think about all this?' He paused, as if searching his memory. 'Morag, isn't it?'

'She's behind me one hundred per cent,' Nielson lied. 'She fully agrees with my decision.'

'Look, there must be something we can offer you,' Amlot said, feeling increasingly desperate. 'Better research facilities . . . a couple of new assistants . . . perhaps an advance paper on your work so far.'

Nielson's face was impassive.

'At least think it over,' Amlot almost pleaded. 'Your work is far too important to us. Anything you can think of which might persuade you to stay, I'll consider.'

Nielson rose from his chair. As far as he was concerned, the matter was closed. 'I *have* thought it over, and I've made my decision. There's nothing you can say or do that will possibly change my mind.'

He turned away from Amlot's desk and walked to the door, leaving without another word. Amlot glared after him, his face set in a grim and angry mask.

Several minutes passed before he was able to calm himself. Finally, he picked up the phone and dialled a number. 'Morag?' he said when it was answered. 'It's Derek. Can you meet me at the Cathedral in about half an hour?'

Morag Nielson ran into Derek Amlot's arms as he approached, pulling his head down into a passionate kiss.

Amlot cast his eyes about nervously, aware that there were other people in the vicinity.

'I've missed you,' Morag said.

Amlot managed to detach himself from her embrace, pushing her away gently. 'I only got back late last night,' he pointed out. 'And did you really have to phone me at the office and leave your number? Caroline might have looked it up.'

Morag looked apologetic. 'I'm sorry, but I didn't know what else to do. I had to talk to you. About Douglas, and this Liverpool business. What are we going to do?'

Amlot nodded, his face grim. 'He sounds pretty serious about it. But I'm prepared to offer him another twelve thousand a year, and increased research facilities. Whatever it takes, basically.'

'Will it work?' Morag wanted to know.

Amlot managed to put more confidence into his voice than he actually felt. 'Look, don't worry. There's no way I'm going to let him go to Landsberg. Not with the knowledge he has locked up in that too-clever little brain of his.'

Morag seemed slightly pacified. 'I'm more concerned about us,' she said, clutching at his arm and looking up at him with adoring eyes. 'Can I see you tonight? We could go to a hotel or something.'

Amlot frowned, shaking his head. 'Not tonight. I have to spend some time at home with the kids. They're expecting Daddy to have brought them some presents. You know what it's like.'

It was the wrong thing to say. Early on in her marriage, Morag had known that Douglas was infertile. A child might conceivably have filled the gap she had always sensed in her life. Her face fell. 'No, I don't know what it's like,' she said bitterly. She broke away from him, sulking.

Amlot realised he had hurt her. 'How about tomorrow night?' he suggested, almost as a consolation prize.

Morag thought for a moment. 'I'm supposed to be doing a client's accounts tomorrow night, but I suppose I could get away by nine.'

'Good, that's settled then,' Amlot said, secretly relieved that he would not have to spend the entire evening with her. The affair was beginning to pall, and Morag's constant demands were placing a strain on him. Like her, he had married for money and prospects, and his wife still controlled a large slice of their property and business investments — money which Casco Pharmaceuticals might shortly need to draw upon unless they could come up with the research breakthrough they needed in the next few months.

He bent over and placed a perfunctory kiss on her forehead. 'Don't worry about it for the moment. Douglas won't be dragging you off to Liverpool, not if I have anything to do with it.' He gave Morag a slightly superior smile. 'Scientists are like children and dogs — give them a few presents and they're devoted to you.' He paused, having had another thought and a little unsure of how to phrase it. 'You could always do your bit, you know,' he said at last, finding no more subtle way of putting it. 'Play the loving wife a bit more. Perhaps if you were especially nice to him for a few days, it might put him in a better frame of mind.'

Morag understood what he was getting at only too well. She gave a little shudder of distaste. 'God, you can be a callous bastard sometimes, Derek. You think I can just switch myself on for Douglas after you and I? Besides, I'm not sure if he'd even want me now. Things have gone too far. Sometimes I think he'd be happier tucked up in bed cuddling one of his bloody snakes.'

'Look, I have to get back,' Amlot said abruptly. 'I'll see you tomorrow night, shortly after nine. Can I leave it to you to book a room at the usual hotel?'

Morag responded resignedly. 'Oh, yes, Derek. Leave everything to me. You usually do.' Her eyes followed Amlot as he walked away. Finally, deep in thought, she started to walk back to her car.

Chapter Nine

It was one of those rare nights when Taggart was able to come home at a reasonable hour, eat a properly prepared meal and then relax for the rest of the evening with a good book and a glass or two of even better whisky. He luxuriated in his favourite armchair, enjoying it. It was good to escape from the world of real murder into the realms of fiction – albeit a spy thriller in which the bodies were already piling up like pork chops on a butcher's slab.

Jean put down her 'Blankets for Romania' knitting and wheeled herself towards the door. 'I'm just going to run a bath before bed,' she announced.

Taggart nodded absently, completely absorbed in his book. Jean smiled at him, pleased to see him enjoying such unusual domesticity. She wheeled herself into the bathroom.

Seconds later, a loud, shrill scream snapped Taggart out of his cosy little fictional world. He sat up with a start, dropping the book and slamming the whisky tumbler down on the coffee-table top.

'Jim, there's a spider in the bath,' Jean called out from the bathroom. 'Will you come and get it out for me, please?'

'Aye, all right.' He stood up, bending down to scoop up the cat which had been curled up at his feet and carried it to the bathroom.

Jean looked at him with a puzzled expression on her face. 'What are you doing with Timmy?'

'I thought it was time he earned his crust,' Taggart said. 'I'm going to put him in the bath. Maybe cats think spiders are very small mice.'

Jean shot him a withering glance. 'You're not going to kill it,' she said firmly. 'I want you to catch it and put it outside.'

Reluctantly, Taggart dropped the cat gently on to the floor and peered over the rim of the bath. A large and extremely hairy spider scuttled around furiously, vainly trying to scale the smooth sides of the tub. He regarded it with distaste.

'Have you ever heard the expression "If you wish to live and thrive, let the spider run alive"?' Jean reminded him.

Taggart pulled a face. 'Well, let it run alive then. I don't like touching those things any more than you do,' he complained.

The expression on Jean's face told him that she intended to get her way. With a resigned sigh, Taggart picked up an empty cosmetic jar and bent over the bath, trying to trap the spider for safe disposal.

A large Black Widow spider scuttled nervously around the floor of its glass case as the beam of a powerful flashlight cut through the gloom of the Casco Pharmaceuticals herpetarium, sweeping the room and its contents. All around, the snakes began a chorus of warning, angry hissing as they too sensed the presence of an unwelcome nocturnal predator.

The torch beam finally settled on the electronic security lock of the outer door. A gloved hand rose to the lock, holding a metal chisel. The snakes hissed with renewed nervousness as the sound of the lock being smashed open broke the silence of the night.

Jardine and DC Reid were already on their way out as Taggart arrived at the station in the morning.

'And where do you two think you're going?' he demanded. 'Off on a little jaunt, are we?'

Jardine waved a slip of paper in the air, his face registering a sense of frustration. 'Just another little thing to keep us busy, sir. The Casco Pharmaceuticals lab was broken into last night. It could be the animal lib crowd.'

'What got taken?' Taggart wanted to know.

'Snakes,' DC Reid informed him. 'Highly venomous ones.'

Taggart nodded resignedly. It was serious enough to warrant two officers. He was also somewhat relieved that Jardine had picked up the crime report before he had. Taggart liked snakes even less than he liked spiders.

'All right, you go off and investigate it. I promised to drop in on Annie Gilmour this morning anyway.'

As Jardine and DC Reid left, Taggart turned away from his office in the direction of the mortuary lab, suddenly remembering that the report from the soil analysis boys had been promised first thing.

Dr Nielson fussed around the empty containers in the herpetarium, obviously greatly distressed.

'So, what are you actually missing?' DC Reid asked, making notes in her book.

'Two Saw-Scaled or Carpet vipers, one Eastern Diamond rattlesnake and two Black Mambas,' Nielson told her. 'And also two American Violin spiders.'

'And how dangerous are they?'

Nielson looked grim. 'They're all very dangerous indeed. The lunatic who took them would be very lucky not to get bitten.' He drew her attention to a black, hairy tarantula. 'You see, most people assume that the bigger and hairier the spider is, the more dangerous it is. It's not actually the case. The two which were taken are Brown Recluses — possibly the most deadly spiders in the world.'

'So, whoever took these animals must have known something about them?' DC Reid asked.

Nielson nodded. 'They certainly took the time and trouble to choose the most lethal. The snakes they selected have a definite tendency to be amongst the most aggressive.'

Jackie Reid made a special note of this fact. 'We'd better go round just once more to double-check there are no other nasties missing,' she suggested.

Nodding in agreement, Dr Nielson led the way round the herpetarium for the fourth time.

In the outer lab, Jardine was talking to Christine Gray, who was equally upset about the break-in and theft. Jardine took things gently, easing into his investigation through casual conversation. The fact that Christine was also a very attractive young woman had not escaped his attention.

'I never realised that snake venom could be that useful,' he said as Christine explained some of her work to him.

'Every species has different enzymes. We can separate them out and use them in drugs.'

'Sounds like a dangerous job,' Jardine said. 'Ever been bitten?'

Christine shook her head. 'No, thank goodness. Dr Nielson has, though, just the once. Fortunately, we keep all the relevant anti-venoms.'

'So whoever took the snakes must have had some experience of handling them,' he observed, watching her face for a reaction.

Christine looked surprised. 'What makes you think so?'

'Well, for a start, they weren't taken in their containers,' Jardine pointed out. 'Someone took them out of their cases and transferred them to something else. No one in their right mind would attempt that unless they knew what they were doing.'

Christine nodded thoughtfully. 'You're probably right. I hadn't thought about it.'

Jardine crossed the lab to look more closely at the security lock on the door into the herpetarium. 'Who knew the number code to this door?'

'Only Dr Nielson and myself,' Christine answered. 'But as you can see, the lock was smashed open.'

'And yet our intruder knew exactly where the snakes were kept,' Jardine said. 'There's no sign of any damage or even searching in any other part of the lab.'

A slight frown flickered across Christine Gray's face momentarily. The implication was obvious – that the intruder had been privy to inside information.

Dr Nielson and DC Reid came out of the herpetarium at last, satisfied that they had accounted for all the missing specimens. Jackie Reid read off her list to Jardine.

'So, how valuable would these creatures be?' Jardine asked Nielson. 'Are they particularly rare?'

Nielson shook his head. 'A private collector, or possibly a zoo might pay a few hundred pounds for them. I can think of much safer ways to make money.'

However, it was a possibility Jardine considered worth pursuing further. 'Just supposing that was the motive – where might the thief go to try to dispose of these specimens?' he asked.

Nielson thought for a while. 'I suppose you could check with the reptile house at Glasgow Zoo,' he suggested. 'Ask for Colin Murphy – he's a friend of mine. He used to work here at the lab, as a matter of fact.'

Jardine nodded at Jackie Reid, who made a note in her notebook. 'Well, if there's nothing else you can tell us, we might as well be off,' he said to Nielson. 'It's obviously a possibility that you will receive some sort of correspondence from whoever took these creatures – animal libbers complaining about experimentation or even possibly some sort of ransom demand. If so, you'll of course keep us informed.'

Nielson nodded, although either possibility seemed rather remote to his way of thinking.

Jardine flashed a smile at Christine Gray. 'Perhaps we could have a chance to talk more about your work sometime,' he said. 'It sounds fascinating.'

Jackie Reid grinned as they left the Casco building. 'So we're into snakes and spiders now, are we?' she teased Jardine. 'Is there no end to your dedication to investigative police work?'

Colin Murphy had just finished giving a hands-on demonstration to a bunch of schoolchildren. Slipping a small African python back into its tank, he glanced up at Jardine and DC Reid as they walked in.

'We're closing up now,' he said politely.

Jardine flashed his ID card. 'Detective Sergeant Jardine, DC Reid. We'd like a word with you.'

Murphy regarded him knowingly. 'Don't tell me — it's about those snakes which were taken from Casco.'

Jardine was a little taken aback. 'How do you know about that?'

Murphy smiled. 'Douglas Nielson phoned me. He said you might be over to see me.'

'Can we go inside?' Jardine asked, nodding towards the reptile room. 'You used to work at Casco, I understand. As a lab technician.'

Murphy led the way into the reptile room. 'That's right — up until last year. I prefer it here, though. It's nice meeting people — especially the kids.' He smiled at Jackie Reid. 'Do you like snakes?'

Jackie looked nonplussed. 'I don't know. I've never really thought about it,' she admitted.

Murphy crossed to a glass tank and took the lid off. Reaching inside, he pulled out a three-foot gopher snake and cradled it gently in his arms. 'This is just a harmless rat snake. We bring him out for the kids' handling sessions. Would you like to hold him?'

Murphy thrust the snake forward. Jardine backed off noticeably. Murphy stood in front of Jackie, presenting the snake like a love offering. 'Go on, hold him. He's all right.'

Jackie cast a sideways glance at Jardine, with a slightly superior smirk on her face. She reached out her hands to accept the snake. Murphy laid it gently across her arms.

'Most people think they're slimy, but they're not. They're not even dry, really — sort of in between.'

Jackie looked down at her slithering handful, not quite able to match the young man's obvious enthusiasm.

'See his tongue going in and out like that?' Murphy went on. 'That's his sensing apparatus. He's smelling and tasting you, trying to figure out if you're as harmless as he is.'

'Do you keep any venomous ones?' Jardine asked, eager to steer the conversation back to the reason for their visit.

Murphy shook his head. 'We don't have any here at present. We don't really have the facilities to keep them. Actually, we have an expert from Chester Zoo here at the moment advising us on that.'

'Do you ever get offered snakes by members of the public?' Jardine wanted to know.

'Sometimes,' Murphy admitted. 'I suppose you'd like to know what would happen if someone we didn't know approached us and tried to sell us really venomous snakes?'

'Does it ever happen?' Jardine asked.

Murphy shook his head. 'Not really. If it did, we'd ask a lot of questions, for a start.' He looked at Jackie and the snake, smiling warmly. 'I think he likes you,' he murmured, noting how the gopher snake had coiled itself up contentedly in her arms.

Jackie returned the smile. 'Actually, I think he's rather cute,' she said, responding to the young man's infectious enthusiasm and charming manner. She was rapidly warming to the idea of snakes in general.

Jardine scowled at her. 'Did you ever handle the venomous snakes at the research lab?' he asked, turning back to Colin Murphy.

Murphy grinned sheepishly. 'Actually, Doug Nielson wanted to train me, but I'm too much of a coward. Have you ever seen pictures of people bitten by snakes? Even if you get the anti-venom in time you can still get tissue damage, gangrene, even lose an arm or leg. You don't risk that on a lab technician's wages.'

He broke off, directing his attention to Jackie yet again. 'Would you like to see something *really* venomous?' Without waiting for an answer, Murphy crossed to another glass tank and carefully lifted aside a large rock. Clustered underneath it were a half dozen tiny, brightly coloured green and black frogs.

Jackie peered into the tank. 'They're gorgeous,' she said.

Murphy nodded. 'Gorgeous, but absolutely deadly,' he agreed. 'Poison Arrow frogs. We don't usually have them out here in the main display area. They're considered dangerous enough to be locked away in the breeding room, away from the general public. Actually, they're reasonably safe to handle, providing you haven't got an open cut, or lick your fingers afterwards. Some species have enough venom in them to kill twenty thousand mice.'

That information was the final straw for Jardine. 'Right — well, you will let us know if anyone approaches you with poisonous snakes they want to get rid of?' He turned to Jackie. 'Now, if you can bear to tear yourself away from your cuddly little friend, perhaps we can get on with some police work,' he said, a little testily.

Jackie handed the gopher snake back to Murphy with a smile. 'Thanks for being so helpful.'

'Anytime,' Murphy said generously. 'You could come back for one of the lecture talks on your day off if you like.'

Jackie smiled at him. 'I might just do that.' She followed Jardine back outside.

They walked towards the exit.

'I do wish you would remember that you're a policewoman when we're interviewing people,' Jardine complained, still a little piqued at being shown up with the snake.

Jackie Reid grinned. 'He was lovely. I could have taken him home with me.'

'So I noticed,' Jardine said with heavy sarcasm. 'I suppose you'd have liked to take the snake as well.'

Jackie flashed him a dirty look, but let it pass.

They passed through the exit, unaware that a sinister-looking man with a strangely scarred face was regarding them with unusual interest.

'Excuse me, sir — I have an urgent message for you,' the desk sergeant called out to Taggart as he was about to leave the station on his way to see Annie Gilmour.

Taggart crossed to the desk. 'So be urgent about it,' he snapped.

'They've found those stolen Roman skulls, sir,' the sergeant announced. 'Two kids playing in the park noticed them dumped in a litter bin and thought they were some sort of toys. Apparently it gave them quite a nasty shock when they realised that they weren't.'

'I'll bet it did,' Taggart muttered. 'That's one thing that doesn't crop up on video games.'

'So Dr Andrews asked what you wanted done with them.'

'Have them returned to Professor Hutton at the Hunterian Museum at once,' Taggart instructed. 'Tell him that I'll be along to see him later. I have a call to make first.'

He left the station deep in thought. It seemed as though an earlier theory had proved right. In fact, quite a lot of things were beginning to fall into place.

Annie Gilmour was putting together a floral display for the window as Taggart walked into the shop. He looked at it with disbelief showing on his face. 'St Valentine's Day? We haven't even got Burns Night over yet.'

Annie smiled. 'That's how this business is, Jim. As soon as that's out of the way, it will be Mother's Day. And then Christmas.'

'I was just passing. Thought I'd drop in,' Taggart said casually.

The look on Annie's face told him that she didn't believe him for a second. 'Do you have some news?'

Taggart nodded. 'There have been a couple of developments.' He paused, uncertainly. 'Look — this goes against my better judgement, Annie, but . . .'

'Tell me, Jim,' Annie broke in, urgently.

'One of the bodies could be Janet's height.'

Annie nodded her head. 'Every day I'm more certain,' she murmured.

Taggart shook his head sadly. 'I'm going to feel as hellish as you if we turn out to be wrong, you know.'

Annie gave him a reassuring smile. 'Then we'll feel hellish together.'

Taggart accepted it. 'There's something else. The soil analysis tells us that one of the bodies has been in the ground for about two and a half years. The one we think could be Janet's has been buried for about four years.'

Annie sighed reflectively. 'Four years tomorrow, Jim. Burns Night.' She paused, looking at him pleadingly. 'Jim, I know I shouldn't ask — but will you have dinner with me tomorrow night?'

Taggart looked apologetic. 'Jean's having a Burns Night supper for disabled people, with a piper to match. I should be there.'

Annie nodded understandingly, but Taggart could see the disappointment, and the sheer loneliness, on her face. Again, he responded against his better judgement.

'On the other hand, I don't suppose she'll miss me,' he said impulsively. 'Yes, of course I'll have dinner with you, Annie.'

Annie said nothing, but the gratitude on her face spoke volumes. The anniversaries of Janet's disappearance must be a particular kind of hellishness, Taggart realised.

'Tomorrow night, then.' With a final, friendly smile, Taggart left the shop.

Hutton had already mounted the Roman skulls in a special display cabinet, along with a couple of daggers, some jewellery and pieces of pottery. He regarded the tasteful presentation with pride before turning to Taggart.

'Well, they're back where they belong. I can't thank you enough.'

'Yes, you can,' Taggart told him. 'By giving me two faces I can identify.' Out of the corner of his eye Taggart saw Dr Andrews stroll into the museum, and beckoned him over. 'An old pal of yours,' he said to Hutton.

Andrews grinned broadly, his hand outstretched. 'Peter, you haven't changed a bit. You still look as though you can't afford a decent pair of shoes.'

Hutton shook his old friend's hand warmly. 'I can't, on the sort of money Strathclyde Police are paying me.'

'Well, how about a bonus?' Andrews suggested. Taggart flashed him a baleful glare. 'I have two tickets for the Federation Burns Supper tomorrow night,' Andrews went on. 'Jenny can't go, so how would you like to come along as my guest? If we can't pay you well, at least let us feed you well.'

'He's got important work to do,' Taggart muttered in objection, but no one was listening to him.

'Thanks, I'd love to come,' Hutton said, settling it.

'Tomorrow night, then,' Andrews said. 'Now, I must take a look round this exhibition of yours. Fascinating.'

'I'll join you,' Taggart announced, falling into step with his colleague as he walked across the museum floor.

'Well, it looks as though Peter is happy again,' Andrews observed.

Taggart grunted. 'I wish I was. Still, at least it confirms what we thought. Those skulls were stolen purely and simply to prevent identification of our victims. When the thief found out he had the wrong ones, he just dumped them.'

'And it also proves that your killer is still around,' Andrews pointed out. 'An old trail you thought had gone cold has opened up again. That must give you some encouragement, at least.'

Unconvinced, Taggart could only nod sadly. 'But if we hadn't let it go cold in the first place, maybe the second victim need not have died.'

Andrews smiled sympathetically. 'No one could have looked for Janet Gilmour more than you, Jim. Now at least you know her killer is still out there somewhere — and very anxious to stop Peter Hutton giving his victims identifiable faces.'

Taggart looked grimly thoughtful. 'But that's the very thing I can't understand,' he admitted. 'We're assuming that they were random victims — but if that's true, what can it possibly be that he's afraid of?'

He looked at Andrews, as if waiting for enlightenment. It was not forthcoming. Finally, Taggart voiced the other vague thought that had been buzzing about in his head.

'More to the point, perhaps, is what is he likely to do next?'

Chapter Ten

With typical disregard for his personal appearance, Hutton continued to work on the skull casts in his freshly hired evening suit. Laying on another dollop of modelling clay with a wooden spatula, he smoothed it into position around the area of the cheekbone and stepped back to review the general effect. 'Well, they're looking human, at least,' he said, pleased with himself. 'Tomorrow, we should be able to see what one of them looked like in life.'

Carl Young stepped over to admire his colleague's work. The two heads were, as Hutton had said, looking distinctly realistic, lacking only ears, hair and fine details like lips and nose shape to make them recognisable sculptures.

He looked at Hutton. 'You've done a wonderful job,' he complimented him. A slight frown furrowed his brow. 'You've got clay on your suit.' He picked up a small brush from the work-top and fussed over Hutton's jacket. Unconcerned, Hutton stepped back to one of the heads, making a slight adjustment to the contours of the cheek. 'I'm still not happy with this side of the face.'

Young glanced at his watch. 'Can't it wait till morning? You're going to be late for your Burns Night Supper.'

Hutton sighed, laying down his sculpting knife. 'Yes, you're right as ever, Carl. I suppose I'd better go and show willing.'

'Oh, by the way. This package arrived for you while you were out at the dress-hire shop,' Carl said, producing a small oblong packet from under the work-top.

Hutton wiped his hands on a piece of rag and took the package, tearing the wrapping paper away. Inside was a small, toughened cardboard box. Ripping off one end, Hutton reached inside.

He gave a sudden exclamation of pain, pulling his hand out of the box in a sudden reflex action. He stared at his finger, where a tiny bubble of blood was already starting to trickle out. He transferred the finger to his mouth, sucking at the wound.

'What's the matter?' Young asked, concerned.

Hutton frowned. 'Must have pricked my finger on a damned staple or something.' He picked up the box again and stared into it. 'That's odd. There's nothing in here – just some wood shavings.'

Young took the box from his hand and upended it, tipping a small pile of shavings on to the work-top. Hutton was right. The box was otherwise empty.

Hutton shrugged. 'Oh, well, I haven't got time to worry about it now. I'd better get to this blasted Burns Supper. See you in the morning.'

Still sucking his finger, which was extremely painful for such a tiny wound, Hutton left the lab.

Hutton felt out of place in the plush surroundings of the huge banqueting room which had been hired for the Burns Supper. For once he was uncomfortably aware that the suit he had hired was not a particularly good fit, and compared to the other guests all dressed up in their kilts and finery, he seemed almost scruffy.

He fiddled nervously with the tight collar of his dress shirt, feeling distinctly ill at ease. The room seemed uncomfortably hot, almost claustrophobic in atmosphere. Hutton wondered, briefly, if he was about to go down with a bout of flu.

Dr Andrews headed towards him, towing Superintendent McVitie in his wake. 'Do you know Peter, Superintendent McVitie? Peter Hutton is working on the reconstruction of the skulls, as you're probably aware.'

McVitie extended his hand. 'Glad to have the pleasure. I hear the work's progressing well.'

Hutton accepted the handshake, noticing that his palms were unusually moist and sweaty. 'Yes, I'm getting there,' he said politely. He felt perspiration prickle out on his brow. 'Is it just me, or is it uncommonly hot in here?' he asked Andrews.

Andrews shrugged carelessly. 'I think they sometimes go a bit over the top with the central heating.'

'Tell me, how do you go about producing the ears and nose?' McVitie was asking. 'That must be the most difficult part.'

Hutton was starting to shiver, like a man with the plague. His head was throbbing, and his knees felt distinctly weak. McVitie's face seemed to swim in his vision, the man's voice coming as though from somewhere far away.

'Yes, most difficult,' Hutton managed to stammer out. He blinked several times, trying to clear his rapidly blurring vision.

'Are you feeling all right?' Andrews asked, concerned.

Hutton forced a brave face. 'Think I might be coming down with the blasted flu.'

McVitie waved his whisky glass with a smile. 'A few of these will soon take care of it.'

'Ladies and gentlemen — will you please take your seats,' came a sudden announcement over the PA system.

'Ah, they're ready to pipe in the haggis,' Andrews said cheerfully. He laid his arm lightly around Hutton's shoulder. 'Come on, Peter. You'll probably feel better when you're sitting down.'

He escorted Hutton over to his table, finding his place-setting for him. Hutton sat down, gratefully, propping his arms on the table and making a bridge of his hands to rest his chin on.

Locking his hands caused a wave of pain which started in his injured finger and seemed to travel all the way up his arm. Through misty eyes, Hutton stared at the offending finger, which now appeared to be quite badly swollen. The area all around the original tiny cut was now blistered and red-looking.

A skirl of pipes welcomed the ceremonial haggis into the banqueting hall, borne on a silver platter. The toastmaster rose to his feet. 'Pray silence for the Address to the Haggis.' He began to intone the traditional ode.

Hutton suddenly felt very nauseous indeed. A shudder ran through his body and he realised that he was on the point of vomiting. With a considerable effort, he managed to push himself to his feet, only to find that his legs no longer seemed capable of supporting the weight of his body.

The banqueting hall seemed to dissolve into a blur of light and sound and swirling shapes. Hutton toppled sideways, crashing against the side of his chair and taking it to the floor with him.

For a moment there was a stunned silence. The toastmaster dried up halfway through his recital. Then a woman screamed, and a babble of excited voices broke out.

Above the mêlée, Dr Andrews' voice boomed out in a commanding tone. 'Someone call an ambulance — at once!'

He ran to Hutton's collapsed form, kneeling beside him and starting to loosen his collar. His old friend was still breathing, but Andrews had not spent all his years with death without realising that Peter Hutton was very close to it.

Just out of the line of Andrews' vision, a small, brown, featureless spider wriggled out of Hutton's warm jacket pocket where it had been hiding ever since biting him nearly two hours previously. Almost invisible against the parquet flooring, it scuttled away to find another refuge.

Taggart and Annie sat facing each other across the table, which Annie had decorated with flowers.

Taggart raised his wine-glass in a toast. 'Here's to the most courageous woman I know.'

Annie shook her head. 'I'm not brave, Jim. It's just that you can't go on pretending that she'll walk in through the door, because she won't. And you can't go on blaming yourself, either. I did it for the first year. That's what killed Ken. He tortured himself to death feeling guilty for driving her out of the house that night.'

Taggart nodded sympathetically. 'Aye, Annie. Life is for the living. We have to get on with it as best we can.'

Annie rose to her feet, suddenly. 'I forgot the table napkins,' she said, with a false sense of urgency which didn't quite ring true.

Taggart watched her dash towards the kitchen and rose from the table, following her. He found her leaning over the kitchen sink, sobbing uncontrollably.

She turned as she sensed him behind her, made one last and desperate attempt to hold back the flood of tears, and then fell forward into his arms. 'Oh, Jim — I do try. I try so hard. And it works, most of the time.'

There was really nothing to be said. Nothing which could possibly do any good. Taggart merely hugged her, offering what comfort he could as the years of pain and bitterness welled up anew and demanded release.

Inside the ambulance, Hutton struggled weakly against the oxygen mask clamped over his mouth, trying to speak.

Dr Andrews bent close to his friend's face, lifting the face-mask slightly and straining to hear the faint words.

'The box,' Hutton was mumbling. 'Something in the box.'

Andrews didn't understand, assuming that Hutton was just rambling in delirium. He placed the mask back into position and lifted the man's hand gently, staring at the red and blistered swelling on his finger. 'It looks like a bite or a sting of some kind,' he observed to the ambulance attendant.

Chapter Eleven

'Sorry to pull you away from your supper with Annie Gilmour, sir,' Jardine said as Taggart arrived at the hospital. 'But I thought that this was important.'

It was a wild understatement as far as Taggart was concerned. 'How is he?'

Jardine shook his head unhappily. 'Not very good, I'm afraid. They have him in intensive care at the moment, but he's virtually comatose. Apparently he was still semi-conscious and delirious when they brought him in, but now he is just about hanging on by a thread. Anyway, Dr Andrews is waiting inside. He was with Hutton at the time he collapsed and he came in the ambulance with him. He might have some more information.'

'Then what are we waiting for?' Taggart snapped. He leapt up the steps to the hospital entrance.

Andrews paced up and down the small waiting-room. He looked up as Taggart and Jardine entered, his face grim.

'Well?' Taggart asked.

'No news yet. But it doesn't look good, Jim.'

'Did he say anything to you. Anything at all?' Taggart demanded.

'Nothing that made any sense,' Andrews answered. 'He was babbling something about a box, but there was nothing in his pockets.'

The waiting-room door opened again. Taggart, Jardine and Andrews virtually pounced together at the young doctor who entered the room.

'Well, it's definitely a bite of some kind,' the doctor announced. 'But I've never heard of such a small wound causing such an extreme reaction. Unless he has a very strong allergy to something, of course. What was he doing, exactly?'

'He was at a Burns Supper,' Taggart muttered, sounding sarcastic without really meaning to.

'Well, obviously, it's important that we find out exactly what we're dealing with here,' the doctor said. 'His vital signs are bad, and I really have no idea of how to treat him. What makes it worse is the fact that I can't access his recent medical records. He was living in the United States until two weeks ago, apparently.'

'When you say a bite — what sort of a bite do you mean?' Jardine put in. 'Could it be from a snake, for instance?'

The doctor shook his head. 'Far too small. The original puncture marks are more like those of an insect — although the inflammation around the wound would definitely suggest the injection of some kind of poison.'

'How about a spider?' Jardine suggested.

The doctor nodded thoughtfully. 'Yes, that's a strong possibility.'

Jardine and Taggart exchanged a sudden meaningful glance.

'Something in a box,' Taggart murmured. 'But he had no box with him.'

Jardine was already thinking along the same lines. 'So it will be wherever he was just before he went to the Burns Supper.'

Andrews overheard the conversation. 'I noticed that he had

smudges of clay on his dinner jacket,' he put in. 'Perhaps he came straight from his lab.'

Taggart nodded. It all seemed to fit. 'Come on,' he said to Jardine. 'Let's see a little bit of that advanced driver's course of yours. Hutton's lab — as fast as you can make it.'

Carl Young pointed to the small cardboard box, still lying on Hutton's work-top where he had left it. 'That's it. It arrived in the afternoon. It appeared to contain nothing more than wood shavings. Peter reckoned he must have jabbed his finger on a staple.'

Taggart regarded the box, then cast a suggestive glance in Jardine's direction. 'Well, you're not expecting *me* to open it.'

Jardine took a pen from his pocket and poked at the box tentatively. 'No staples,' he pointed out. He lifted the loose flap of the lid gently and peered inside. Finally, satisfied that there was nothing moving inside, he upturned it and emptied out the last few wood shavings on to the work-top.

'You noticed nothing?' Taggart said to Carl Young.

The man shook his head. 'No, like I told you, I was clearing up. I heard him call out, then he dropped the box to the floor — just about where you're standing right now.'

Taggart took a couple of steps backwards, rather hurriedly.

Jardine was examining the wood shavings. 'Sir — these shavings. I'd say they were identical to the ones in the spider tank at Casco.'

Taggart glanced around anxiously. 'Come on, let's get out of here,' he suggested. 'That thing could still be crawling about somewhere.'

'It'll probably turn up in a corner, frightened,' Jardine muttered.

Taggart grimaced. 'I don't care how it feels.' He moved towards the door, casting nervous glances around the floor as he walked.

They returned to the car.

'That chap at Casco — the poisons expert you saw about the break-in. What was his name?' Taggart asked.

'Dr Nielson, sir,' Jardine said. 'And he's a toxinologist, or so I'm told.'

In the urgency of the moment, Taggart ignored Jardine's rather smug correction. 'Well, whatever he is — get to him as fast as you can and find out whether he holds an antidote for the bite of that spider. And order a car to get me back to the hospital, and I'll meet you there.'

Jardine climbed into the car and set the blue light flashing. He drove off with a squeal of brakes, spraying gravel from the drive over Taggart's shoes.

Taggart looked surprised when Jardine turned up at the hospital with Christine Gray. She held a small plastic phial in her hand.

'I couldn't get hold of Dr Nielson,' Jardine explained hurriedly. 'Luckily, I remembered Christine, who also had a key to the anti-venom store.'

'Is that it?' Taggart asked, looking at the phial.

Christine nodded.

'Let's hope we're not too late,' Taggart said, taking it from her hand and heading for the intensive care unit. He returned a few moments later.

'So you have a key to the Casco building, and also to the anti-venom store?' he quizzed Christine. 'What about the room where they keep the snakes and creepy-crawlies? Do you have a key to that as well?'

'No — just Dr Nielson, the research director — and of course the security staff,' she answered.

Taggart nodded to himself thoughtfully, remembering the smashed lock on the herpetarium door. For the time being, he decided not to press the matter any further. 'Well, you'd better see about getting the young lady home,' he told Jardine. 'There's not much more we can do here except wait — and hope.'

Christine smiled at Jardine. 'Not another high-speed chase through red traffic lights with sirens and blue lights flashing,' she said. 'I don't think I could take any more excitement tonight.'

Taggart gave her a withering look, nodding his head in the direction of the intensive care unit where Peter Hutton was fighting for his life. 'It wasn't very exciting for him,' he pointed out rather gruffly.

Jardine put his arm protectively around Christine's shoulders. 'Come on, I'll get you home.' He steered her towards the door, pausing when they were out of Taggart's earshot. 'Unless you'd like to stop off somewhere for a drink, that is,' he added.

Christine beamed. 'Yes, I'd like that.'

Jardine looked pleased with himself. 'There's a rather nice new wine bar that's just opened up quite near here,' he suggested. 'How about that?'

Christine clutched at his arm, almost possessively. 'That would be super,' she murmured, looking up at him happily.

Nielson carried two pints from the bar over to the table where Colin Murphy sat waiting.

'Thanks for meeting me, Colin,' he said quietly. 'I just felt like talking to an old friend tonight.'

Murphy sipped at his pint. 'So, Morag has walked out on you?' he said without a great deal of sympathy.

'She says she wants some time to think things over,' Nielson said, nodding miserably. 'She's going to stay in a hotel for a few days — or so she says.'

'I don't know why you let her control your life the way you do,' Murphy said. 'You know you ought to take that job in Liverpool. You'll kick yourself if you don't.'

Nielson smiled ruefully. 'Life isn't that simple, Colin. You're not married.'

'I wouldn't want to be married — not if it meant having a woman tell me what I could and couldn't do,' Murphy said firmly. 'I think you ought to do what she suggested — get a flat in Liverpool and come home at the weekends.'

'That's just what she'd like,' Nielson said bitterly. 'But I'm not going to give her the satisfaction of doing exactly what she wants, without me in the way to stop her.'

'You mean — other men?' Murphy looked shocked for a while,

then grinned suggestively. 'Have you ever . . . you know . . . had other girls?'

Nielson stared into his glass, morosely, saying nothing.

'Don't you get jealous?' Murphy asked after a while. 'If I was married, and I thought my wife was playing around, I know what I would do.'

Nielson regarded the younger man with a rather condescending smile. 'What, kill her? Don't think I haven't considered it.'

Murphy's eyes glinted with excitement. 'Would you do it the way you told me once?' he asked. 'You know — with snake venom?'

Nielson looked a little rattled. 'I don't remember ever telling you about that.'

'You were a bit drunk once,' Murphy reminded him. 'You told me how you had worked out the plan for a perfect murder — injecting cobra venom into someone's belly-button.'

Nielson frowned. 'Oh, that was just the beer talking,' he said, annoyed with himself at the stupid indiscretion. 'Besides — you'd still have the problem of keeping your victim still while you did it.' He smiled suddenly, quickly changing the subject. 'Look, there's an office party at Casco tomorrow night. A girl from Allergies and a new chap from Anti-Fertility are getting engaged. Why don't you come over as my guest? We could sink a few jars together.'

Murphy thought about it for a few seconds. 'Yes, I might just do that,' he said after a while. 'I'll see how I feel.'

Nielson finished off his pint and rose to leave. 'Well, I'd better get home. Another pint and I'll be over the limit. So I might see you tomorrow, then?'

Murphy seemed disappointed that Nielson was going. Despite the difference in their ages he had always enjoyed his company. 'I'll let you know in the morning,' he promised.

Nielson noticed the police car parked in his driveway as he arrived home, and felt a distinct sense of unease. He had sunk at least three pints, and he wasn't sure if he could safely pass a breathalyser test. He switched off the ignition and stepped out of his car, sucking in deep breaths of the fresh night air to clear beer fumes from his mouth and lungs.

Taggart stepped out of the car to greet Nielson as he walked towards his front door. The man looked nervous, almost guilty, he thought. 'Dr Nielson! We have a man seriously ill in hospital. We believe he was bitten by one of the poisonous spiders stolen from your lab.'

Nielson looked flustered. 'I don't know what to say,' he murmured, uncertainly.

'You could start with "how is he",' Taggart suggested.

'Yes, of course.' Nielson collected his thoughts. 'You'll need the anti-venom, and quickly. We can pick it up from my lab.'

'Already taken care of. My colleague picked up Christine Gray, your assistant,' Taggart informed him. He established eye-to-eye contact. 'You weren't at home tonight.'

There was something about Taggart's manner that made the simple statement sound almost like an accusation. Nielson fidgeted nervously. 'Look, you'd better come in,' he murmured, fishing in his pocket for his door key. He opened the door and led the way into the house.

'So — where were you?' Taggart wanted to know after they had seated themselves in the lounge.

'I . . . I went out for a drink with an old friend. I needed someone to talk to about a personal problem.' Nielson watched Taggart's face, wondering if the basic explanation would suffice. Obviously, it would not. 'I've been offered a new job — in Liverpool. My wife doesn't want to leave Glasgow,' Nielson expanded.

Taggart's impassive expression flickered with the faintest trace of sympathy. 'This friend — do you mind telling me his name? Her name?'

'A man. An old work colleague,' Nielson said emphatically. 'Colin Murphy — he works in the reptile house at the zoo now. I wanted to invite him to a party tomorrow night.'

'Party?' Taggart jumped on the word.

Nielson frowned. 'Just an office celebration. Colin used to work at Casco as a lab technician. Look, what's this all about? Why are you asking me all these questions?'

Taggart declined to give him an answer. Instead, he posed another question, albeit rhetorically. 'I assume that everyone in the Casco building knows about your little menagerie.'

Nielson's eyes narrowed. 'Are you implying that it was a member of the staff who stole the snakes and spiders?'

'A possibility, wouldn't you think?' Taggart fired back.

Nielson shook his head. 'No, frankly, I wouldn't.'

Taggart spelled it out for him. 'Frankly, Dr Nielson — someone knew where they were, exactly which ones to take, and how to handle them. Now, I don't know about you, but I don't care for sheer coincidence.'

Nielson fell silent, unable to think of a suitable rejoinder.

'Tell me, did you ever know a girl called Janet Gilmour?' Taggart asked suddenly.

For a second Nielson was nonplussed, unable to follow the abrupt jump in Taggart's line of questioning. 'You mean the missing girl who was in the papers?' he queried eventually. 'No, of course not. Why should I know her? More to point — why do you ask?'

Again, Taggart refused to give him a straight answer. 'It's just that someone seems very anxious to prevent us identifying a skull that might be hers,' he said. He rose to his feet, pausing as if with a sudden afterthought. 'Oh, Dr Nielson. You said you were having wife troubles. Where is your wife tonight, by the way?'

Nielson's face clouded over with repressed anger. 'You tell me,' he said bitterly. 'You're the bloody detective.'

Morag Nielson's face was still slightly flushed from the pleasures of love-making. She turned her head sideways on the pillow, admiring Derek Amlot's handsome face. He looked worried.

'What is it, Derek?' she asked softly.

Amlot chewed at his bottom lip nervously. 'I'm not sure that walking out on Douglas was such a good idea.'

Morag smiled, snuggling up closer to his warm body. 'I haven't exactly walked out on him. I just panicked him a little. If he thinks he's going to lose me because of this, he'll stay.'

Amlot was not totally convinced. 'I just hope you're right,' he muttered. 'I'd give anything to stop those bastards at Landsberg getting their hands on Douglas's research.'

'Don't worry,' Morag reassured him. She kissed his cheek. 'Can you stay the night? Make some excuse that you've been called away on business?'

Amlot shook his head. 'Not tonight. It's Denise's birthday. I promised I'd take her out to a nightclub.'

Morag pulled away from, him with a petulant expression on her face. 'So I end up playing second fiddle again.'

Amlot sighed heavily. 'Look, we've been through all this. We both know the rules.'

But Morag was not to be mollified. 'Damn the rules,' she spat angrily. 'Perhaps I wouldn't mind playing second fiddle so much if you weren't always the conductor. Sometimes I feel that you're only using me as a means to keep Douglas at Casco.'

Amlot forced a reassuring smile on to his face. He rolled across the bed, cuddling her. 'You know that isn't true,' he whispered in her ear. 'Look, we'll meet again tomorrow.'

Morag turned her face away, hiding the tears which were beginning to prick out in the corners of her eyes. 'I seem to spend my bloody life waiting for tomorrow,' she murmured bitterly.

Jean Taggart also seemed to spend a great deal of her life waiting for a man who was supposed to be part of her world. There was a sad, almost resigned look on her face as her husband entered the house. Wrongly, he assumed it was merely because he had missed her Burns Supper evening.

'Look, Jean — I'm sorry,' he said. 'But it certainly really has been one of those nights. How was the supper, anyway?'

Jean fought back her tears. 'Timmy got killed,' she said in a flat, emotionless voice. 'He ran out into the road and a car hit him. We buried him in the garden. Apart from that, and you not being there, it was just fine.'

Taggart felt her pain, and his face screwed up in anguish. 'Aw, Jean — I'm sorry,' he said lamely, knowing as he spoke that it was not enough, but conscious of the communications void which had grown up between them. He knelt beside her wheelchair and lightly kissed her hair. 'Come on,' he said gently. 'I'll see you up to your bed.'

Chapter Twelve

Dr Andrews was waiting for Taggart in his office, his face grave and drawn.

'Hutton?' Taggart said, using the gut instinct he had developed over the years.

Andrews nodded sadly. 'He died during the night. Apparently, serious complications can arise in some cases. From what I can glean, the venom went to his kidneys which became necrotic. A tragic end for such a brilliant man. I'm sorry, Jim.'

Taggart sighed resignedly. 'I'm sorry for you, Stephen. I know he was a friend.'

Andrews shrugged. 'It was a long time ago. We really didn't have a great deal in common. He was a homosexual, you know.'

Taggart accepted this information stoically. He had suspected as much. 'His assistant, Carl Young?'

Andrews nodded. 'Someone had better tell him, I suppose.'

'Jardine's with him at the moment,' Taggart volunteered. 'Checking on how far he had got with the reconstruction work.

Probably not far enough, unfortunately.'

'So you're back at square one?' Andrews sympathised. 'No other leads? Any possible connection between this research lab and Janet Gilmour?'

Taggart shook his head. 'Nothing so far. I'll have Mike Jardine ask around tonight — he's going to gatecrash a little party at Casco.'

Carl Young paused at the door to Hutton's workroom, the key poised but unturned in the lock. 'Are you sure it's safe in there now?'

'So I'm told,' Jardine assured him. 'The experts say that those spiders are used to a warmer climate. They couldn't survive forty-eight hours of Glasgow weather.'

Young turned the key in the lock and opened the door. Despite Jardine's reassurance, he kept his eyes on the floor as he walked across to the work-top where the two clay busts stood.

Jardine looked at them with disappointment. Neither was yet recognisable as a human face.

'How long is Peter likely to be in hospital?' Young asked.

Jardine shrugged. 'I have no idea. Too long for us, unfortunately.'

'I could always carry on where he left off,' Young suggested. 'I mean, the basic structure is all there. It's now just a matter of sculpting the facial features.'

It seemed a slim ray of hope, but Jardine jumped at it. 'Do you really think you could do it? How much experience do you have?'

'I've done facial constructions on several ape-man skulls,' Young said. 'Admittedly that was more guesswork than these need to be — but I've worked with Peter for a long time now and I've always studied his work closely. I helped him with the heads-in-a-trunk case in America. I'd certainly welcome the chance to prove I could do it.'

The man's confidence was encouraging. Jardine was tempted to give him the go-ahead on the spot. Then he remembered Taggart's words: 'Use your intitiative — but keep me informed.'

84

'I'll have to check it out with my chief,' Jardine said cautiously. 'Can I use your phone?'

'Help yourself,' Young said, gesturing across the room to it.

Jardine picked up the phone and dialled Taggart's direct number. 'It's me, sir. I'm in Hutton's work lab. His assistant has just come up with a rather interesting proposition.'

Taggart listened as Jardine explained. 'He really seems that confident?' he asked at length.

'We really don't have much to lose, sir,' Jardine pointed out. 'Even if he makes a mess of it, we still have the original skulls. Hutton can try again when he recovers.'

'We don't have that luxury any more,' Taggart told him bluntly. He filled Jardine in with the details of Hutton's death. 'So, Young is our last hope,' he explained finally. 'We can't afford to blow it. I want round-the-clock protection for him, and this whole thing kept under tight wraps. As far as the rest of the world is concerned, Peter Hutton didn't even *have* an assistant. Our maniac has to think that the work on the skulls has gone elsewhere.'

'I understand, sir,' Jardine said. 'I suppose you want me to break the news?'

'Aye, but do it gently,' Taggart told him. 'Hutton had a very special relationship with Carl Young, according to Dr Andrews.'

The news came as a surprise, but not a shock. Jardine did not let his chief in on this fact. 'Leave it to me, sir,' he said simply.

'Oh, and by the way. Get out your dancing shoes,' Taggart said, oddly.

This time Jardine was thrown, and it showed. 'Sir?'

'You and DC Reid are going to a party tonight. At Casco's. I want you both there with your eyes and your ears open. Speak to everyone — find out if anyone ever had any contact with Janet Gilmour.'

'But they'll know who we are, sir,' Jardine objected.

'So? People drink at parties. They get drunk and talk. You'll let them — and you'll be very good listeners.' Taggart hung up the phone.

Jardine turned to Carl Young. 'I'm sorry, but I have some very bad news for you. I'm afraid Peter Hutton died during the night. There was nothing anyone could do.'

Young stared at him blankly for several seconds. Then his eyes began to mist over with tears. Jardine averted his gaze, slightly embarrassed without fully understanding why.

To his credit, the young man composed himself quickly. He moved over to the skulls, brushing them gently and almost lovingly with his fingertips. 'I'll do a good job for you,' he promised Jardine, in a soft but firm voice. 'It will be my tribute to Peter. He was a very great man.'

Jardine regarded his date for the night through new eyes, secretly impressed. He had seen Jackie Reid in civilian clothes before, but not dressed up in full party finery. She looked quite stunning.

'I hope you realise we're not here to enjoy ourselves,' he said as they climbed out of the taxi outside the Casco building.

Jackie Reid glared at him. For a rare change she was feeling like a woman and not just a junior police officer. Although she hadn't really expected a compliment, it might have been nice. 'With a little bit more effort, you could sound like Jim Taggart,' she said cuttingly.

Whatever his shortcomings regarding salaries and working conditions, Derek Amlot was no Scrooge when it came to allocating funds for the company social fund. The Social Club had been transformed for the evening and given a more than adequate budget to lay on a really good party. There was a generous and varied buffet laid out along one wall of the room, a professional-looking disco unit complete with flashing lights and wide-screen video effects, and the small but functional bar was dispensing free drinks for the evening.

Feeling slightly embarrassed as an outsider, Jardine pushed his way through to the bar and ordered drinks — an orange juice for Jackie and a non-alcoholic lager for himself.

Having been served, they both edged along to the end of the bar and stood with their backs to it, establishing a vantage point from which to observe the scene around them.

If Jardine had hoped to remain a discreet, detached observer, it was not to be. Drink in one hand, and a piece of half-eaten quiche in the other, Angus Mackay flounced over towards them, flamboyant as ever.

In party mood, he was dressed outrageously, even by his usual dandyish standards. In mustard-coloured trousers, with a maroon blazer and an oversized spotted silk bow-tie worn on a frilled dress shirt, he reminded Jackie Reid of a hatless Mad Hatter, straight out of the Tenniel drawing.

'Ah, our pair of gatecrashers,' Mackay announced in a voice which would have served well as a public address system. 'Our dearly beloved director of research said you'd be here. Have you seen the lovely Maureen, by the way — or is she off picking pockets somewhere? She steals everything else around here.' Mackay dropped his piece of quiche on the bar and held out a limp hand to Jardine, who shook it reluctantly. 'Angus Mackay, Allergies Department. Also a veritable mine of inside information. Looking for a murderer? Try Dennis over there — he tries to poison everybody with his foul cups of tea.'

Jardine glanced over in the direction which Mackay had indicated. The young man in question stood alone in a corner, looking lost, lonely and even a bit frightened by all the noise and activity around him. Much more interestingly, Nielson and Colin Murphy sat together at a nearby table, which was littered with empty pint glasses.

Jardine nudged Jackie as discreetly as he could, trying to draw her attention to the pair. Unfortunately, he was not quite as discreet as he intended to be. Mackay followed the direction of his gaze.

'Oh, I shouldn't bother trying to talk to Douglas,' the man gushed. 'He's already pissed as a fart.' He grinned waspishly. 'Tell you what — someone should have sent that spider to poor old Nielson's wife. That might have been a practical solution to his problems.'

Jardine was beginning to get very annoyed with the man. He placed his glass down on the counter and slipped his arm around

Jackie's trim waist. 'Shall we dance?' he suggested, pulling her away from the bar.

Taken slightly by surprise, Jackie put up no resistance as Jardine led her on to the small dance floor.

Jardine pulled her body close to his, dropping his lips to the level of her ear. 'Don't worry – this isn't a sudden romantic urge. I just needed to get away from that dreadful man. Nielson and Murphy are over there, and I think we ought to try to get to talk to them. In a minute, you hover near their table and see if you can get Murphy to notice you. You appeared to have a mutual attraction to each other last time you met, I seem to remember.'

'And who will you be talking to?' Jackie fired back. 'The nubile Miss Gray, I presume?'

'I didn't realise Christine was here,' Jardine lied. She had been the first person he had looked out for when they came in.

Somewhat clumsily, Jardine manoeuvred them across the dance floor towards Nielson and Murphy's table, eyeing the two men discreetly. Mackay had been absolutely right in one thing – Nielson was quite obviously drunk. Although Jardine could not yet pick out individual words in their conversation, Nielson's tone had that unmistakable self-pitying whine of a man in the throes of alcoholic depression.

Murphy, on the other hand, seemed agitated, excitable. Jardine edged nearer to the table, straining his ears above the loud disco music to eavesdrop on the conversation.

'She treats you like shit, Douglas,' Murphy was saying. 'I can see it, everyone else here can see it. You should go round to the hotel where she's staying right now – have it out with her.'

Nielson stared morosely into his half-empty glass. 'She'd only accuse me of spying on her. She'd say I'd come expecting to find her with someone. Don't want to give her the satisfaction.'

Murphy got to his feet. 'You're a fool to yourself, Douglas. She isn't worth it. Come on, I'll buy you another drink.'

He started to walk in the direction of the bar. Jardine saw their chance. 'Right, you go and say hello to Nielson,' he instructed Jackie Reid. 'That way you'll be there naturally when Murphy comes back.' Taking her off the dance floor, he looked around for Christine.

She, in turn, had just noticed Colin Murphy and was moving to intercept him on his way to the bar. Jardine smiled inwardly with satisfaction, pleased with himself for his sense of timing. Two birds with one stone.

She was greeting Murphy warmly as Jardine approached.

'Colin, how lovely to see you. I didn't know you were going to be here.'

Murphy basked in her smile. 'Douglas invited me. I thought it would be nice to come back and see you all.'

'Hello again,' Jardine said to both of them. 'I didn't realise you two knew each other.'

Murphy seemed to resent his intrusion. He turned to Christine. 'Is this your new boyfriend?'

Christine didn't seem too sure. Mike Jardine had in fact broached the subject of them meeting again, but nothing definite had been arranged. She decided to cover her bets. 'No — not really. We had a drink last night — after that terrible business with the spider.' Thinking about it again, Christine gave a little shudder. 'Ugh, that poor man. How is he, by the way?'

'I'm sorry, didn't you know? He died during the night. The anti-venom couldn't save him, unfortunately.'

Christine looked shocked. 'I'm sorry. I had no idea.' Her sad expression changed to a puzzled frown. 'That's very strange, though. It's usually pretty effective if administered within five hours.'

'Yes, well . . .' Jardine shrugged non-committally. 'Some sort of complications, apparently.'

Murphy had only just recognised Jardine. 'Oh, you're the policeman who came to see me about the snakes. Did you find them, by the way?'

It was a naïve and rather stupid question, Jardine thought. He was unnecessarily sarcastic in his answer. 'No, but we know where one of the spiders was last night.'

Jardine's tone carried a clear message, which Murphy could not fail to receive. He waved the empty glasses he was carrying, smiling rather sheepishly at Christine. 'Well, I'd better get to the bar. I promised Douglas I'd buy him a drink.'

Jardine considered pointing out that Nielson looked as though he had already had more than enough, but kept quiet. He didn't really want to give the young man any excuse to hang around any longer.

Christine regarded him with a faintly chiding expression as Murphy excused himself and left. 'You were a bit rude,' she pointed out.

'Yes, I know. I'm sorry,' Jardine said. He wasn't really sure why he had been quite so antagonistic towards Colin Murphy.

But if he failed to understand, Christine Gray thought that she had the answer. She smiled up at Jardine. 'He's not a boyfriend or anything like that, you know. He used to work here, that's all. I mean, he's quite sweet and all that, but I don't fancy him or anything.'

For some reason it embarrassed Jardine to think that he was acting like a stag in rut. 'The thought hadn't crossed my mind,' he said, aware that he was lying both to her and to himself.

Christine grasped his arm. 'Would you like to dance with me?'

Jardine nodded, a little relieved to let her make the running for the time being. They moved on to the dance floor. 'You were going to tell me more about your work,' Jardine said, making conversation. 'What is it you're working on, exactly?'

'Basically, I'm trying to grow venom cells from the glands of dead snakes,' Christine explained. 'That way, it won't be necessary to catch live snakes and then milk them.'

'It sounds a lot safer,' Jardine observed.

'And more productive,' Christine added. 'Milking venom is a slow process, and it makes the production of anti-venoms expensive. If my project succeeds, it might mean that the people who really need the anti-venoms can actually afford them. It could save thousands of lives each year.'

'How's that?' Jardine asked.

'It's mostly poor peasants and field-workers in the Third World who die from snakebites. Either their employers are too mean, or unscrupulous dealers push the price of the anti-venoms up beyond their reach.'

'So, it's valuable work?' Jardine said. 'And what about Dr Nielson – what's he working on?'

Christine looked a little awkward. 'I'm not supposed to talk about that to anyone,' she said, almost apologetically. 'His research is rather secret – and potentially worth a great deal of money. That's why they don't want him to leave.'

Jardine decided to push just a little bit further. 'When you say a great deal of money, what sort of figures are we talking about?' he wanted to know. 'Thousands . . . millions?'

'Millions, certainly,' Christine admitted. 'If research results in a commercially viable drug which passes all its clinical testing stages, it can be virtually priceless.'

It was food for thought, and more than sufficient motive for murder, Jardine realised – although what possible connection there could be between Nielson's research and Hutton's death remained a total enigma, even assuming that there was any connection at all. He sensed that Christine was beginning to get a bit fed up with being quizzed about her work, and changed the subject. 'Shall we go and get something to eat?' he suggested.

On their way to the buffet table, Jardine noted that Jackie Reid had succeeded in dragging Colin Murphy away from Nielson and had him pinned in a corner. Nielson himself was now slumped across the table, well into his cups.

'Do you think we should go and see if Dr Nielson is all right?' Christine asked, concernedly, noticing him. 'Poor man, he must be under so much strain lately, what with making such a big decision about his career and now this trouble with his wife.'

'Trouble?' Jardine's ears pricked up. This was something he hadn't heard about.

Christine nodded. 'There's a rumour going about that she's left him. Some people have even suggested that she's having an affair with Derek Amlot, our managing director.'

'Quite a little hotbed of gossip, this place,' Jardine observed.

'And what about Nielson himself? Any little scandals concerning his private life?'

Christine bristled protectively. 'Dr Nielson is a fine man. I'm sure he has done nothing wrong at all.'

Jardine should have heard the warning bells, but he didn't. Unwisely, he continued probing. 'No stories about other women . . . girls? Did he ever know a girl by the name of Janet Gilmour, for instance?'

Christine suddenly looked very disappointed. She stopped in her tracks, gazing at Jardine. 'You're not really interested in me at all, are you?' she asked flatly.

Jardine was caught off guard. The brief moment when he might have been able to bluff it through came up, and passed. His slightly flustered expression was enough of an answer for Christine.

'You just want to pump me for information,' she said coldly. 'You're just another bloody policeman.'

She walked off, leaving Jardine cursing himself for his clumsiness. At a loose end, he walked over to Jackie Reid and Colin Murphy.

'Colin was just telling me how to commit the perfect murder,' Jackie said as he joined them. 'He thought we might come across it one day in our work. It seems that what you do is fill a hypodermic with cobra venom and inject it into your victim's belly-button.'

'You see, cobra venom is almost impossible to detect unless you're actually looking for it,' Murphy put in, obviously highly pleased to have gained Jackie's interest. 'And if there was an autopsy, the last place they would look for a puncture is in the navel.'

'Very interesting,' Jardine muttered. 'I suppose Dr Nielson told you about this?'

Murphy nodded. 'He taught me a lot of interesting things when I was working here. He's a nice man.'

'So I'm finding out,' Jardine said, more to himself than anyone else.

Murphy glanced across at Nielson, slumped across the table.

'Actually, I think I'd better take him home.'

Christine came over, making a beeline for Murphy. Pointedly ignoring Jardine, she clutched at his arm. 'Are you going to dance with me, Colin?'

Murphy shook his head regretfully. 'I'd better get Douglas home. He's in a bad way.'

'I'll come with you,' Christine offered impulsively. 'You might need some help.' She steered him away in the direction of Nielson's table.

Jackie Reid looked at Jardine with the faintest trace of annoyance on her face. 'Well, you seem to have achieved your objective of us not enjoying ourselves. What now?'

Jardine looked sheepish. 'I suppose we'd better find some more people who are willing to talk to us,' he suggested.

Murphy pulled his car to a halt in Nielson's drive and turned to the man sprawled across his back seat. 'Here we are, Douglas. Safely home.'

Sitting beside him, Christine looked up at the house. An upstairs bedroom light suddenly snapped off. 'I think your wife's home, Dr Nielson,' she said. 'I just saw a light go off.'

Nielson groaned. The last thing he felt up to coping with was a flaming row with Morag. He groped for the car door handle, opening it with some difficulty and staggering out. His eyes roved drunkenly around the driveway. 'She can't be home — her car's not here,' he slurred.

'Well, I definitely saw a light go out,' Christine said.

Murphy got out to help prop Nielson up as he lolled against the side of the car. 'Come on, Douglas, I'll give you a hand to the front door.'

'Why don't you both come in for a nightcap?' Nielson suggested.

Murphy shook his head. 'No thanks. You need your bed, Douglas.' He walked Nielson across the drive to the front door and helped him fit his key into the lock.

Pushing Nielson in through the opened door, Murphy pulled it shut and walked back to the car. Before starting it up, he turned to Christine. 'How about you coming back to my place for a while?'

Christine thought about it for a second. She had wanted to make Jardine feel jealous, but there was no point in taking things too far.

'No thanks, Colin,' she said finally. 'I think I'd rather get straight home.'

'I cook a really good spaghetti bolognese,' Murphy offered as an extra inducement.

Christine laughed. 'What, after quiche and pizza? You must have a lead-lined stomach.'

'Just a drink, then?' Murphy suggested, unwilling to let her go without trying everything.

Christine leaned across and kissed him on the cheek. 'You're very sweet, Colin — but I really do feel quite tired,' she told him.

Murphy shrugged resignedly and gave her a good-natured grin. 'Well, you can't blame me for trying, can you?'

Christine squeezed his arm. 'No, of course I don't blame you for trying. Perhaps another night, eh?'

'Sure,' Murphy nodded, turning the ignition key in the lock. He cast one last look up at Nielson's house before driving off. The upstairs lights had gone on. Nielson was obviously taking his advice and going straight to bed.

Nielson lurched into his bedroom, fumbling for the light switch on the wall. The room seemed unnaturally warm. Even in his drunken state Nielson could feel waves of heat emanating from the nearby radiator.

There was something vaguely disquieting about this fact, and the actual temperature of the room seemed to remind him of something, but Nielson's brain wasn't functioning at full capacity.

Carelessly, he stripped off his clothes and dropped them in an untidy pile on the floor. As he undressed, he had another vague and uneasy feeling that he had heard the front door open and close, but it seemed too much of an effort to investigate.

Without bothering to put on his pyjamas, Nielson climbed into bed and reached up to switch off the overhead reading light. Suddenly, he froze.

Something cold was moving against his bare flesh. Something not dry, not slimy, but strangely in between. It was of a temperature and a texture that he recognised only too well.

Nielson's body convulsed with shock. Suddenly, he remembered what the temperature of the bedroom had reminded him of. It was the herpetarium in his lab. He panicked, even though logic told him it was the one thing he should not do. But logic was already swamped by instinct — far older and far better established in the human psyche. Shuddering with horror, he tried to scramble out of the bed, but it was too late. A sudden, piercing pain in his side caused him to scream out in agony.

With a reflex action, Nielson threw back the bed covers, clutching his hands over the source of the pain. His terrified eyes fell upon the large Black Mamba which was sharing his bed, its ugly mouth opened wide and residual venom still dripping from its gleaming fangs.

The snake struck again, biting him on the thigh. Nielson screamed in sheer terror, thrashing out wildly with his legs and arms in a vain attempt to drive the deadly creature away.

It was useless. Under attack, the Mamba responded by striking repeatedly, even after it had exhausted its full reservoir of venom. By the time it bit him for the fifth time, Nielson no longer felt any pain from its sharp fangs sinking into his flesh. There was a greater, more urgent pain on the left-hand side of his chest, like a hot knife being twisted inside him. There was a roaring, rushing sound in his head. The reading light above his head seemed to flare suddenly into blinding white intensity, like a star going super-nova.

Then blackness descended — a total all-enveloping darkness which dropped over him like a thick and stifling blanket.

Nielson's body gave one final, convulsive shudder, and then lay still.

Chapter Thirteen

The whole area around Nielson's house was already cordoned off as Jardine drove up in response to Taggart's message over his car radio.

Getting out, he walked over to join Taggart and Superintendent McVitie outside the front door of the house. 'I got on to Christine Gray, sir,' Jardine announced. 'She wasn't too happy about coming out on her own, but luckily there's a venomous snake expert on loan to Glasgow Zoo at the moment. He's already on his way.' Jardine broke off, nodding at the front door. 'So what happened?'

'Nobody knows yet,' Taggart told him. 'The morning cleaning lady found Nielson in his bed, saw the snake and panicked. No one's been back into the house since. The place could be crawling with 'em. Have you tracked down Nielson's wife yet?'

'She's staying at the County Hotel, sir. Marital tiff, apparently.'

McVitie grunted. 'Some tiff. You'd better bring her in for questioning, Jim.'

'I'll send DC Reid, sir,' Taggart said, looking over towards Jackie, who was still trying to comfort the near-hysterical cleaning lady. 'Another female might get more of an instinctive reaction from her.'

McVitie raised his eyebrows slightly. In all the years he had known Jim Taggart, it was the first time he had ever heard the man admit that women police officers might have special talents.

'Ah, Dr Andrews is here,' Jardine announced as another car pulled into the drive.

Andrews hurried across and went to open the front door. Taggart stopped him. 'I wouldn't go in there if I were you,' he warned.

'But we don't know if he's dead yet.' Andrews said.

Taggart shrugged. 'Not for sure, no — but I'm damned if I'm playing John Wayne to find out.'

'It's probably more afraid of us than we are of it,' Andrews suggested.

Taggart was not convinced. He nodded across to the distraught cleaning lady. 'Tell her that,' he muttered. His eyes were suddenly drawn by the sight of two officers wearing flak jackets and carrying shotguns. 'What's the SWAT team doing here?'

'It comes under the official definition of wild animals, Jim,' McVitie told him. 'Standard procedure.'

'And no doubt more official standard paperwork,' Taggart muttered sarcastically. He looked over to the entrance to the drive as a small van drove up and was stopped by a pair of officers. 'Who's that?'

'It'll be the snake expert from the zoo I expect, sir,' Jardine said. 'Shall I give permission to let him through?'

'Aye,' Taggart nodded. 'The sooner it's safe to go in that house, the better.'

Jardine waved across to the officers. The van pulled into the drive, parking behind Jardine's car.

Taggart walked over to meet the man who stepped out, noticing that his face and chin were oddly scarred, although some attempt at skin grafting had obviously been attempted. 'You the reptile man?'

The man nodded, grinning. 'Well, I'm not the Slime Beast From Hell. Name's Sullivan. I understand you have a little snake problem here.'

'Aye, you could say that,' Taggart murmured. He looked at the man's hands, expecting to see protective gloves, but they were bare. 'Are you going in there like that?' he said, in surprise.

Sullivan smiled easily. 'Oh, snakes are all right if you know how to handle them. I'll just get my gear from the back of the van.' Opening the back doors, he took out a large cloth bag and a pair of long-handled tongs.

'That's it?' Taggart said, even more amazed.

Sullivan nodded. 'That's it. Now, where is our little beauty?'

Taggart gestured towards the front door. 'Last seen in the bedroom — but it could be anywhere by now.'

'Then it's probably still there,' Sullivan said confidently. 'Snakes don't like to move around too much, unless they're hungry or something startles them.' Pushing past Taggart and McVitie, he went into the house.

He was out again in less than five minutes, holding the cloth bag which was now bulging. He held it aloft like a trophy.

'Here you are. One of the mysteries of life locked up in those venom glands. It's as if each snake had man in mind as an enemy as it evolved a capacity for storing venom.' Sullivan jerked his head, gesturing back into the house. 'He's quite dead. It's unusual for a snake to kill outright. Sometimes it's the shock that does it. I've seen a man die of a heart attack after being bitten by a harmless gopher snake.'

'Thanks for the autopsy,' Taggart snapped. 'Now, is it safe for us to go in there?'

Sullivan nodded. 'I had a look round. Couldn't see any others. It looks like someone broke in through a window at the back.'

Still slightly dubious, Taggart led the way into the house, closely followed by Andrews, Jardine and McVitie.

Andrews cast a cursory glance over Nielson's body, sprawled out on the bed. 'He's been bitten five times,' he observed. 'Nothing could have saved him.' He broke off, bending down to pick something up from the bed. He held it up — a piece of sloughed-off snake skin. 'This should interest you.'

Taggart didn't need to be told what it was. 'You mean it was in bed with him?' he said with a faint shudder.

'It would appear so,' Andrews said.

'They like warm, dark places,' Jardine volunteered. 'He'd have settled down and stayed there contentedly until he felt cornered. Then he'd strike, repeatedly.'

Taggart noticed the unusually high temperature in the room. 'Why is it so hot in here?'

'My guess is that the killer turned the heating up so the snake would remain active,' Andrews suggested.

Jardine had found a cardboard box over the other side of the bed. He looked inside it very carefully, eventually lifting out another larger piece of snake skin. 'I think I've found what it was brought to the house in,' he announced.

'Put it back,' Taggart snapped. 'And put it on the list for the fingerprint boys when they get here.' He looked at Andrews. 'Can I leave things here to you now?'

'I'll do a more thorough examination before we move him,' Andrews said. 'But I don't think there's going to be any radical developments for a while.'

Taggart gestured to Jardine. 'Come on — let's go and see this Murphy character. According to you he was the last person to see Nielson alive.'

The look on Murphy's face told Jardine that he already knew about Nielson's death.

'You've heard, then?'

The young man nodded sadly. 'Christine phoned me.' He looked up at Taggart, as though worried. 'That was all right, wasn't it? I mean, she won't get into trouble or anything?'

'No, she won't get into trouble,' Taggart assured him. 'Now, tell us exactly what happened when you took Nielson home last night.'

Murphy shrugged. There wasn't much to tell. 'We dropped him off, and that was about it. We didn't go into the house with him because we didn't want to get involved in his marital problems.'

'But you knew his wife had left him and was staying in a hotel?' Jardine put in.

'She must have come back,' Murphy said. 'There was a bedroom light on upstairs.'

'How do you know it was his wife?' Taggart asked.

Murphy shrugged again. 'Who else could it have been? Mind you, Douglas did say that her car wasn't there – so maybe it wasn't.'

'So you're telling us that there was definitely someone else in that house when you left?' Taggart recapitulated.

Murphy nodded. 'That's right. You can ask Christine – in fact, it was her who saw the light go off.'

'Don't worry, we will,' vowed Taggart. 'Because if she doesn't back you up, it means that you were the last person to see Nielson alive. Whoever killed him knew how to handle snakes – and where the most venomous ones were kept in the Casco lab. You qualify, on both counts.'

Murphy looked shocked. 'Come on – you can't think I killed Douglas. He was a friend.'

'Last night – you were telling us an interesting little story about how to commit a perfect murder – with snake venom,' Jardine put in.

'I told you – that was something Nielson told me about, ages ago,' Murphy protested. 'I don't even know if it works.'

'Now why should Dr Nielson tell you how to commit a murder?' Taggart wanted to know.

'It was just a joke,' Murphy said, but the look on his face told Taggart that he was hiding something.

'A joke?' he repeated, with heavy emphasis. His eyes bored into Murphy's.

Murphy looked resigned. 'Well, I thought it was a joke at the time. It was another period when he was having trouble with his wife. He was fantasising about ways to kill her without getting caught.' Murphy broke off as if a sudden thought had struck him.

He turned towards Jardine. 'You don't suppose she got to him first, do you?'

It was certainly something to consider, Taggart reflected as he and Jardine walked back to the car. But then there were plenty of other things to consider as well.

'Two scientists dead. Both top men in their fields. Now, is there anything in that?' he asked Jardine.

Jardine thought about it for a while. 'Well, Nielson was a research boffin,' he muttered eventually. 'I learned last night that his work was potentially worth millions to his company. And they're probably not too keen on losing one of their top people — especially to their biggest competitors.'

'So, in a way, we could say that Casco would be one of the main beneficiaries of Nielson's death?' Taggart mused. 'They already have the benefits of his work so far, and there's no chance of a rival company capitalising on the information inside his head.'

Jardine nodded. 'That's about the strength of it, sir.' He suddenly remembered the other fascinating bit of gossip he had gleaned at the party. 'Oh, and one other little snippet I picked up last night, sir. There's a rumour going around that Casco's managing director, Derek Amlot, has been having an affair with Nielson's wife.'

Taggart found this information most interesting. He paused, with his hand on the door handle of the car, looking at Jardine with a thoughtful look on his face. 'I think Mr Derek Amlot is most definitely our next customer,' he said firmly.

Chapter Fourteen

In fact, Taggart was wrong. There was another customer already in the queue before Derek Amlot. She was waiting for him in one of the interview rooms when he and Jardine returned to the station.

Taggart decided to let her wait a bit longer, heading for McVitie's office instead. DC Reid was already there, looking pleased with herself.

'I've brought Morag Nielson in for questioning, sir,' she announced. 'She may be a bit rattled. I caught her in *flagrante delicto,* as it were.'

Taggart scowled at her. 'Aw, give it to us in plain English,' he grumbled.

Jackie Reid wiped the smile off her face. 'She was engaged in sexual activity,' she reported. 'They were doing it as I walked in. Nielson's wife and Derek Amlot, the managing director of Casco Pharmaceuticals.'

'A proper little nest of vipers we have here,' McVitie observed laconically.

Taggart merely grunted. 'And how did you manage to interrupt this romantic little scene?' he asked DC Reid.

'I persuaded one of the chambermaids to open the door with her pass key,' Jackie told him. 'There was a "Do Not Disturb" notice on the door handle, but it accidentally dropped off while I was examining it.'

Taggart smiled thinly. 'How clumsy of you,' he muttered, belying the implied compliment for the young officer's initiative. Jackie Reid's face glowed with pride.

'Anyway, I brought her in, sir,' she continued. 'But Mr Amlot had to return to work.'

'And you let him go?' Taggart's complimentary mood hadn't lasted very long.

'He was very forceful, sir,' Jackie protested. 'He said he had a very important business meeting with two Indian gentlemen.'

'To discuss what? The Kama Sutra?' McVitie put in with untypical humour.

The joke fell a little flat as Jardine chose that precise moment to knock on the door and enter. 'Carl Young has just phoned to say that one of the faces is ready for photographing,' he announced. He paused, suddenly realising that he had broken in on a discussion of some sort. 'Sorry, have I interrupted something?'

Taggart smiled, nodding at DC Reid. 'No, but she did, I'm happy to say. We have Nielson's wife in for questioning. I suggest you and DC Reid go and see what she has to say for herself.'

Morag Nielson was not even attempting to play the part of the grieving wife. She glowered at Jardine and Jackie Reid as they walked into the interview room. 'How much longer are you going to keep me here?' she demanded angrily.

'Until we're satisfied that you have told us everything we need to know,' Jardine informed her.

'I already made a statement to one of your junior officers,' Morag muttered peevishly. 'What more do you want?' She took a cigarette out of a silver case and lit it, her fingers trembling slightly and betraying the nervousness underlying her bravado.

'Did you want your husband dead?' Jardine asked suddenly.

Morag eyed him coolly. 'No, he was a good provider,' she said in a flat, virtually emotionless voice. 'I'd be a fool to want it all taken away, wouldn't I?'

'Yet you were having an affair with his boss,' Jardine pointed out. 'No doubt Derek Amlot would be an even better provider.'

Morag's eyes flashed fire. 'Derek has a wife and family, whom he won't leave. You can't lay that one at my door.'

'Why the hotel?' Jackie Reid put in.

Morag flashed her a bitchy, withering glance. 'I should have thought that was obvious when you barged in. Or do women detectives only get to write about it in their little notebooks?' She returned her gaze to Jardine, appealing to him. 'Look, I'm the grieving widow, remember? No one's even told me yet how Douglas died. When are you going to stop asking me all these questions?'

Jardine was unmoved by the woman's feminine appeal. 'I haven't seen much evidence of grief,' he said flatly.

Morag shrugged, realising that she could not manipulate the young man. 'Okay, I'll tell you the plain truth. I was calling his bluff – hoping that Douglas would realise that losing me was more than his new job was worth. It's not a crime to want to hold on to your husband, is it? Besides, I was doing Derek a favour at the same time. The company didn't want to lose Douglas either.'

The interview room door opened quietly and Taggart strode in. Jardine made the formal introductions. 'Mrs Nielson – Detective Chief Inspector Taggart.'

Morag's eyes flickered with new interest. Another, and older, man to practise her charms on. She gave Taggart the full treatment. 'Please, when are you going to tell me how Douglas died?'

Taggart's face was impassive. 'In our time.'

'I'm his wife, I have a right to know,' Morag insisted.

Taggart ignored her. 'Where were you between eleven and twelve o'clock last night?'

Morag thought for a second, then shrugged. 'I can't remember.'

'We have two witnesses who inform us that there was someone upstairs in your house when your husband came home,' Taggart said, watching her eyes carefully.

There was the faintest, momentary flicker of worry.

'Well, it wasn't me,' Morag said.

'So where were you?' Taggart demanded, not letting her off the hook.

Morag had recovered herself again. 'You give me a straight answer and I'll give you one.'

Jardine glanced at Taggart, who gave him a faint, almost imperceptible nod.

'Someone put a venomous snake in your husband's bed,' Jardine told her. 'It bit him five times and he suffered a heart attack.'

For the first time, Morag's composure broke. She shuddered, a look of genuine horror crossing her attractive face. 'My God — I still sleep with him. It could have been me.'

Taggart and Jardine exchanged a brief glance, both registering disappointment. The woman's obvious shock had been too spontaneous, too genuine.

Jackie Reid could not resist putting in her own cutting comment. 'I wonder if he would have known the difference,' she murmured.

There was a long silence, which Taggart finally broke with a resigned sigh. 'Well, that'll be all for now, Mrs Nielson. You can go, but we might need to speak to you again.'

'Do you think there'll be any point in talking to her again, sir?' Jardine asked after Morag Nielson had left.

Taggart shook his head. 'I doubt it. If that one was going to commit a murder, she'd want to do it personally.'

Jardine nodded. Taggart had summed up his own views perfectly. 'Well, I suppose we'd better go and see what sort of a job Carl Young has done with that face,' he suggested.

'You go on ahead,' Taggart told him. 'I'm going to pop round and pick up Annie Gilmour. I think she deserves the right to see it first, before we splash it all over the newspapers. I'll meet you there.'

'Need a woman's touch, sir?' DC Reid offered.

Taggart shook his head. 'No thanks. I've carried this one for four years. I'll see it through.'

Jardine and Carl Young stood aside almost deferentially as Taggart showed Annie Gilmour in. The clay bust stood alone on a table across the room. Tactfully, Carl Young had put away the original skulls and other reminders of death which normally littered the lab.

Annie walked slowly across the room towards the table, her eyes firmly fixed on the sculpted head. Reaching it, she gazed for what seemed an eternity to Taggart and Jardine, saying nothing.

Finally, she quietly drew up a nearby chair and sat down, staring at the bust from eye level. Still silent, she reached out and touched it, stroking the hair lovingly with her fingertips.

Without looking round, she spoke for the first time. 'That's her,' she murmured in a low, level tone. 'That's my Janet.'

Taggart moved across the room and stood beside her. Stooping slightly, he laid one arm gently across the woman's shoulders. 'No doubts, Annie?' he asked softly.

Annie shook her head, without taking her eyes off the clay head. 'The hair isn't quite as she used to wear it . . . and her face was a little fuller . . . but it's my Janet.'

She half-turned, looking up at Taggart. Her eyes were misty, but they shone with gratitude. 'Thank you, Jim. Thank you for bringing her back to me.'

For once Taggart was at a loss for words. He merely hugged her momentarily, then stepped back, leaving her to continue staring at the bust of her beloved daughter.

Derek Amlot was on the defensive from the moment his secretary showed Taggart and Jardine into his office. As often happens with men used to wielding power, this manifested itself in an arrogant, almost aggressive, façade. He showed them to a pair of designer armchairs and sat down behind his large, rather ostentatious desk.

'Look — this must be rather embarrassing for all of us,' he started, eager to establish himself as the top businessman rather than the casual adulterer.

Taggart shot a sideways glance at Jardine, then faced Amlot again, his face a mask of innocent surprise. 'Oh, it's not embarrassing for me . . . or him,' he assured Amlot.

The man averted his eyes, fiddling with an expensive-looking executive toy on his desk. 'What would you like to know?'

'For a start, how many of your scientists' wives you've been to bed with,' Taggart snapped.

Amlot's discomfiture increased. He picked up a photograph of his wife and children, displaying it. 'I have a wife and family. They're very important to me. I'm happy with them,' he said, as though it were some sort of explanation.

'What was Dr Nielson working on?' Jardine put in suddenly.

Amlot's eyes narrowed. 'Is that relevant?'

'If it wasn't, I wouldn't have asked,' Jardine said simply.

Amlot returned the photograph to the desk, as if realising that it was not going to be some kind of magic talisman to protect him from interrogation. 'Research consultants are very much their own people — free to work on whatever projects they like,' he explained. 'Sometimes neither I nor even Mrs MacDonald, our research director, know exactly what it is they are doing.'

'But it was something important?' Jardine pushed.

'All scientific research is important,' Amlot responded.

'Suppose he was on the verge of a really important breakthrough?' Taggart postulated, taking up his colleague's line. 'Losing him to Landsberg would be quite a blow.'

'Are you suggesting that he was killed for that reason?' Amlot asked.

Taggart shrugged. 'I'm not suggesting anything.'

Amlot formed a church and steeple with his hands, tapping the spire of his fingers against his lips. 'Look, poaching scientists is nothing out of the ordinary. It happens all the time. We've even done it ourselves. Unfortunately, you can't buy loyalty.'

'But maybe you can arrange for it in other ways — like manipulating their wives, for instance,' Taggart muttered.

Abruptly, the conversation was back on the very topic Amlot wished to avoid. He fidgeted nervously. 'Can we bring this meeting to a conclusion? I'm a very busy man. I have an important meeting in a few minutes.'

'Your secretary just kindly cancelled that meeting,' Taggart told him. 'Now, where were you between eleven and twelve o'clock last night? Were you with Mrs Nielson?'

Amlot shook his head. 'I went to the hotel early this morning. Last night I was with my family.'

'So where was Mrs Nielson?' Taggart asked.

'I don't know. I'm not her keeper,' Amlot snapped testily. He paused, suddenly aware of the consequences of his last few statements and adopting a far more conciliatory tone. 'Look, if you're going to check with my family, I'd appreciate a little discretion. We are men of the world, after all.'

Taggart refused to give him the assurance he was seeking, resenting the inference that marital infidelity was merely a harmless game for grown-up little boys. Quite apart from any personal or moral judgement, he had seen the tragic results of it far too often in his professional life. He lifted himself out of the comfortable chair. 'That'll be all for now,' he said, leaving Amlot in no doubt that he was still very much on the hook. He motioned to Jardine and they left the office in silence.

Jardine waited until they were well out of earshot of Amlot's personal secretary. 'Well? What now?'

'Go over to the research lab and see what you can get out of Christine Gray,' Taggart instructed.

Jardine looked at him in surprise. 'Don't you want to talk to her too?'

Taggart grinned, tapping the side of his nose with his fingers. 'I'm going to be a man of the world, Michael.' He broke step, cutting away at a tangent and heading for the main exit.

Dennis and his tea-trolley were again blocking the corridor leading to the toxinology lab. Jardine waited until the last customer had departed. He smiled at Dennis in a friendly fashion. 'I'll take a cup of tea, if there's a spare one going.'

Dennis grinned amiably. 'You're one of the policemen, aren't you? You were at the party last night.'

'That's right,' Jardine said, taking his cup of lukewarm tea. 'Dennis, isn't it?'

The lad nodded, his simple face registering real pleasure that an important person like a policeman would remember his name. 'It was terrible what happened to Dr Nielson,' he said sadly. 'He was really nice to me. He used to let me watch him milk snakes sometimes.'

Jardine sipped at his tea. 'But not handle them, I take it?'

Dennis smiled secretively. 'He did once. There was this Baboon viper which had got cold and hibernated, and he let me touch it. It was nice.'

'You like snakes, do you, Dennis?' Jardine asked conversationally.

Dennis nodded enthusiastically. 'I'd like one as a pet,' he said, his face glowing at the thought of it. Then he looked sad again. 'But my mum wouldn't let me have one, I know.'

Jardine finished his tea. 'Well, that's prejudice for you,' he observed. He placed his empty cup back on the trolley. 'Well, it was nice talking to you, Dennis. And thanks for the tea.'

He walked away with yet another piece of jigsaw puzzle in his mind. A retarded young man who liked snakes. Jardine turned into the toxinology lab, still wondering if it had any significance at all.

Christine Gray looked up from her microscope as Jardine entered the lab. She regarded him coolly. 'I wondered when you'd come,' she said simply.

Jardine sighed, getting the message loud and clear. 'Look, I need to talk to you about the work that Dr Nielson was doing,' he said, almost apologetically. 'I know you were reticent last night, but things are different now.'

Christine stood up, gesturing across the lab towards a large filing cabinet. Two of the drawers had been pulled out and left open.

'When I got in this morning, every file relating to Dr Nielson's project had been removed,' she said. 'Even his personal notebooks are missing.'

'Amlot?' Jardine asked.

Christine shrugged. 'Derek Amlot ... Maureen MacDonald ... they probably want to know exactly the same things as you do.'

The telephone rang. Christine picked it up and listened for a few seconds. 'Just a minute,' she said to the caller. Wrapping her hand over the mouthpiece, she whispered to Jardine. 'Talk of the devil. Dr MacDonald wants me over in Derek Amlot's office right away.'

Jardine snatched the telephone from her hand. 'This is Detective Sergeant Jardine. I am talking to Miss Gray on police business,' he snapped into the mouthpiece.

Maureen MacDonald did not seem impressed. 'Well, this is company business,' she retorted. 'Dr Nielson's death has caused a number of urgent problems which have to be dealt with swiftly.'

Jardine was about to protest when Christine gently pulled the phone away from him. 'I'll be over in five minutes,' she said, replacing the receiver on the hook. She looked up at Jardine. 'It's probably best that I play ball with them. I can always give you that statement you need later, if that's all right.'

Jardine thought about it, realising that the situation had, in fact, provided him with an ideal opportunity to try to patch things up with Christine. The annoyed frown on his face faded away, to be replaced by a hopeful smile. 'How about this evening?' he suggested. 'I could come round to your house after you finish work. Perhaps we could go for a drink or something?'

'Fine,' Christine said in a matter-of-fact tone. She didn't sound terribly enthusiastic.

She probably wasn't going to give him a second chance, Jardine realised rather sadly. Cursing himself yet again for his clumsiness, he left her collecting her notes together for the meeting and walked silently out of the lab. Rather belatedly, he was realising that he had quite fallen for Christine Gray.

Chapter Fifteen

Taggart walked slowly through the cemetery grounds, heading for a specific grave. As he had expected, Annie Gilmour was already there, sitting on the grass with a small bunch of flowers in her hand, gazing silently at the headstone.

She did not turn round as he walked up behind her. Taggart read the inscription on the stone, as he had many times before: 'May The Peace of Knowing Pass Beyond Life'.

'I thought I'd find you here,' he said softly, standing above her. 'The shop was closed up and you weren't at home.'

Annie spoke without looking up, recognising Taggart's voice. 'I just didn't feel like facing the public today. I made a promise to Ken just before he died. I said I'd come and tell him the day we found her.'

She laid the flowers at the foot of the grave and started to get up. Taggart helped her to her feet. 'You've kept that promise, Annie,' he said gently.

Annie smiled distantly. 'Aye, as much as you can keep a promise to the dead. Maybe he'll lie in peace now.'

She turned away from the grave and began to walk slowly back towards the cemetery entrance. Taggart fell into step beside her. 'Annie – did Janet have anything to do with a company called Casco Pharmaceuticals?' he asked. 'Did she ever mention it? Did she know anyone who worked there?'

Annie thought deeply for a while, finally shaking her head. 'Not that I can think of. But then Janet didn't tell me everything about her life.'

'I can't help thinking that there was a whole part of her life that we never discovered,' Taggart murmured. 'Something which would have given us a whole new perspective – new avenues of investigation which we never pursued.'

Annie was on the defensive at once. It was an old subject – one that had caused friction with Jim Taggart in the past. 'She never took drugs, Jim. She was never in any kind of trouble. I would have known. Janet was a good girl.'

'Annie, I wasn't necessarily suggesting that,' Taggart was quick to assure her. 'But she must have had secrets which she hid from you and Ken.'

Annie sighed wearily. 'Ah, you were always the cynic, Jim. You could never quite believe that a girl of Janet's age could be so innocent.'

Taggart accepted the criticism without defence. 'It's just that – after a row with her father, she didn't go to her friends, any of the people you might expect her to turn to. She just vanished.'

'And now she's found,' Annie said simply. 'Can't we just leave it at that?' She looked into Taggart's face, his apologetic expression giving her the answer to her question. 'So where does this pharmaceutical company fit it?'

'I'm not even sure that it does,' Taggart admitted. 'It's just a hunch – something which has been bothering me for days.'

Annie changed the subject abruptly. 'That young man who sculpted Janet's face? Could you ask him if I could keep it?'

Taggart shrugged. 'I've no objection. Of course I'll ask him for you.'

Annie gave him a thin smile. 'It was a very strange feeling when I walked into that room.'

Taggart nodded understandingly. 'It must have been.'

'As though . . . as though she'd never really been missing at all,' Annie murmured, an odd look in her eyes.

Taggart flashed her a puzzled expression, not understanding. They had reached the cemetery gates. Taggart's car was parked just outside. 'Would you like me to give you a lift home?' he offered.

Annie shook her head. 'No, I'd like to walk for a bit, if you don't mind, Jim.'

'Sure, Annie,' Taggart said. He gave her a reassuring smile. 'It'll be all right, Annie. It will be easier now.'

He walked to his car, wondering whether Annie believed it any more than he did.

Christine Gray glanced sideways out through the window of Derek Amlot's office. It was already getting dark. She checked her watch, amazed to find that the 'debriefing', as Dr MacDonald had called it, had gone on for more than five hours.

'Is this going on for much longer?' she complained to Amlot. 'I didn't even get a lunch break. I'm tired and I'm hungry.'

Amlot cast a sideways questioning look at Maureen MacDonald, who nodded faintly. He began to scoop up the sheaf of papers, notes and files which littered his desk. 'No, I think that will take care of everything, Christine. You've been very helpful. Thank you. Dr Nielson was very fortunate to have you as his research assistant.'

'There's one more thing before I go,' Christine said. She pulled a sealed letter from her lab coat pocket and dropped it on to Amlot's desk. 'I don't feel that I can carry on working here without Dr Nielson. We were very much a team — and, had he left, I would have gone with him. I've written a formal letter of resignation.'

Amlot's face registered concern. 'What about your own project? Have you thought of that?'

Christine's face was set. 'I've considered everything.'

Amlot glanced up at Maureen MacDonald, appealing for her help. 'Can you talk some sense into her?' he asked.

Maureen adopted a friendly woman-to-woman tone. It seemed

strangely out of keeping with her normal personality. 'Your project is very important, Christine. Snakes are very expensive to buy and to keep. Being able to produce venom cells in the laboratory from dead glands could save us thousands.'

'To say nothing of revolutionising work with natural toxins,' Amlot put in. 'Your work here could carry considerable prestige in the scientific world. I'm prepared to renegotiate your contract on far more favourable terms.'

Maureen picked up the envelope, holding it out to Christine. 'Look, why don't you take this back and think about things a little more,' she suggested. 'After all, we're scientists. We don't do things in haste.'

Christine took back the envelope grudgingly. 'All right, I'll consider your offer,' she said to Amlot. 'But I feel I must warn you — I don't think I shall be changing my mind.'

She stood up to leave, missing the anxious, almost desperate look which passed between Maureen MacDonald and Derek Amlot.

Taggart locked his car and began to walk up the path towards his front door. Suddenly he froze, his stomach turning to ice. On the doorstep was a large cardboard box, almost identical to the one which had been found in Nielson's bedroom.

Taggart forced his legs to move, taking a few more tentative steps towards the box. Stopping about three feet short, he strained his eyes in the dark to pick out any distinguishing marks on the box. Even as he stared the box moved — almost imperceptibly, but it was a movement nevertheless.

Taggart felt the hairs on the back of his neck prickle. His mouth was dry. He backed away slowly for three or four feet and then turned, breaking into a run for his car and the radiophone inside.

The house was cordoned off as though in the throes of a siege, as Jardine arrived on the scene. He headed straight for Taggart, who stood regarding the spotlights, armed officers and general activity with a sullen glare. He had recovered from his initial fear now, and was merely very, very angry. This was his home, his sanctuary. Taggart felt a sense of violation.

'Good job you were vigilant, sir,' Jardine said.

Taggart shot him a withering glance. 'I could hardly miss the bloody thing, could I?'

'Where's Jean? Is she all right?'

'Out, luckily,' Taggart said. The thought of his wife opening the box in all innocence made him shiver with cold rage.

'I take it you've already sent for Sullivan?' Jardine asked.

'Too right,' Taggart said, with heavy emphasis. 'I called him before I called you. So we wait.'

'How did you get on with Mrs Amlot, by the way?' Jardine asked, to relieve the frustration of waiting more than anything else.

'She confirmed her husband's story — of course,' Taggart told him. 'And Christine Gray?'

Jardine filled him in with the basic details. 'In fact, I was at her house when I received your call,' he finished up. 'She wasn't in, so I'll go back later.'

Another police car drew up outside the cordon. Sullivan stepped out, holding his rubber-capped tongs and cloth bag. Recognising him, Taggart waved him through the police guard.

'Right — where's your problem this time?' Sullivan said cheerily.

Taggart regarded him with a scowl, then pointed to the box. 'In that. I saw it move.'

'You didn't look inside, I take it?' Sullivan said, the faintest trace of a smile playing on his lips.

'Are you kidding?' Taggart almost exploded. 'Suicide isn't fashionable this month.'

'Right — let's take a little look,' Sullivan said, advancing up the path towards the front door.

'Excuse me, sir. Mrs Taggart's here,' one of the constables called out.

Taggart looked round to see Jean's invalid car just drawing up behind the line of police cars. He nudged Jardine gently in the ribs. 'Go and keep her calm, Michael.'

As Jardine moved off, Taggart returned his eyes to the unfolding drama. Sullivan had reached the box now, and was carefully prodding it with the end of the tongs. Very slowly, he prised open the top flap and bent over it, peering inside.

Taggart could feel his heart pounding with the tension of it all. Suddenly, his jaw fell slackly open with sheer dismay as Sullivan dropped the tongs on to the path and reached inside the box with his bare hands. Taggart's stomach knotted as the man's arms disappeared inside the box.

They emerged — bearing a small, fluffy and extremely nervous little kitten. Sullivan carried it down the path ceremoniously and presented it to Taggart with a huge grin on his face. 'Here, I think this is for you.'

Taggart fervently wished the earth to open and swallow him up. His entire being positively seethed with embarrassment. For a moment he half expected Sullivan to suddenly tear off his disguise and reveal himself as Jeremy Beadle.

With monumental unwillingness he let Sullivan place the kitten in his arms. Turning away from the house, he marched towards Jardine, who was helping Jean out of her car.

Without a word, Taggart dropped the kitten into Jean's lap. Her face beamed with pleasure. 'Oh, how cute. Mrs McIvor up the road must have left it for me. Her cat had a litter, and she heard about poor Timmy.'

Taggart left her admiring the kitten. He pulled Jardine away by the sleeve, glaring up at his face and searching for the faintest sign of a grin. 'Don't you ever . . . ever . . . mention this again,' he warned.

To his credit, Jardine kept a perfectly straight face. It took almost superhuman effort.

Chapter Sixteen

Jardine was waiting in his car for Christine Gray when she finally arrived back at her flat, exhausted after the long session with Amlot and Dr MacDonald and another hour of collecting together what notes she could for Jardine.

She was not pleased to see him, and it showed.

Jardine got out and walked towards her as she locked her car doors then walked round to the back and opened the hatch, lifting out her small terrier dog and placing it on the pavement. She closed the hatch and locked it, looking up at him with a tired, pleading look in her eyes. 'I don't suppose this can wait until tomorrow?'

Jardine shook his head apologetically. 'Had a hard day?' he sympathised.

Christine turned towards her flat. 'You could say that. Nearly six hours I spent with them. Going through every file, every note. I'm whacked.'

Jardine shuffled his feet awkwardly. 'Look, I'm really sorry, Christine — but this is important. You understand?'

She nodded wearily. 'Yes, of course. You'd better come in.' She led the way up the path to the front door, the dog trotting beside her.

Jardine followed her. 'Do you always take your dog to work with you?' he asked conversationally.

'It's better than leaving him alone in the house all day. This way I can at least let him out during my morning and afternoon tea-breaks.' She opened the door, looking down at the dog. 'You'll be hungry, Brandy. Never mind, I'll get you some dinner in a minute.'

She ushered Jardine into the hallway and closed the door, sealing out the cool night air. The flat was warm and cosy by comparison.

'What about you?' she asked Jardine. 'Do you want a bite to eat?'

Jardine shook his head. 'No thanks. I've eaten already. But you go ahead and make yourself something.'

'Well, if you're sure,' Christine said gratefully. She showed him into the parlour. 'Make yourself comfortable on the couch. I'll get you something to read.'

As Jardine seated himself, she rummaged through a pile of magazines on a small coffee-table, selecting one and handing it to him.

'Only copies of *New Scientist*, I'm afraid,' she apologised. 'But you might find this one interesting. It contains an article on drug research using enzymes in snake venom. With all the credit taken by a certain Dr Maureen MacDonald, would you believe?'

Jardine took the magazine and opened it, finding the article in question and beginning to read. Christine took off her coat and threw it over the back of a chair.

'I won't be five minutes,' she said to him. 'If you're too hot, I'll turn the heating down. It shouldn't be set this high, anyway.'

'No, I'm fine,' Jardine muttered absently, concentrating on the magazine article.

Christine left the room and headed for the kitchen, her dog trotting behind her with its tail wagging furiously in anticipation of food. It headed straight for the food cupboard and began to bark furiously.

Christine looked down at it in surprise. It was unusual for Brandy to make such a fuss. 'You must be really hungry,' she said to the dog. 'Just hold on a second and I'll feed you.'

Christine crossed the kitchen and opened a small transom window. She adjusted the central heating control on the wall nearby and turned back to the still barking dog. 'Right, now to keep you quiet,' she murmured, moving towards the larder door.

In the parlour, the noisy barking of the dog was upsetting Jardine's concentration. He dropped the magazine reluctantly on to the sofa and stood up, absently stripping off his jacket. Christine had been right; the flat was uncomfortably hot.

That sudden realisation hit him like a shock wave. A sense of foreboding rose like bile in his stomach, rapidly escalating into a terrible and very real knowledge of dread. Jardine exploded into action, rushing towards the kitchen screaming out Christine's name at the top of his voice.

She looked up at him in surprise as he burst into the kitchen. She had opened the larder and taken out a large paper sack of dried dog food. 'Whatever is the matter?' she asked anxiously, dipping her hand into the sack.

Jardine never got the chance to tell her. Christine's words ended in a scream of shock and pain. She fell back, scrambling madly on the slippery kitchen lino as she tried to pull herself away from the larder. The paper sack fell over, its contents scattering across the floor. Hissing angrily, a Saw-Scaled viper slithered out through the open mouth of the sack and threshed about on the floor, kept temporarily at bay by the excited, barking dog.

Jardine rushed to Christine, slipping his hands underneath her armpits and dragging her across the kitchen floor to comparative safety. Snatching up a kitchen stool, he advanced towards the snake. 'Don't! Don't try to touch it,' Christine shouted urgently. 'Just pick up my dog if you can.'

Holding the stool out in one hand like a lion-tamer, Jardine managed to scoop the other under the terrier's belly. Lifting the dog to safety, he stepped back hurriedly and threw the stool at the snake, which slithered back into the larder.

Jardine bent over Christine, who had propped herself up against the far kitchen wall. 'Are you bitten?' he asked urgently. Even as he spoke, his eyes fell upon the twin puncture marks on her arm, just above the wrist. 'Oh, Christ!' he cursed helplessly. 'What do I do?'

Christine helped herself to her feet slowly with one hand, trying to keep the bitten arm as still as possible. She was suddenly strangely calm. 'It's important that I don't move around too much,' she told Jardine in a low, matter-of-fact voice. 'It will only help the poison to spread through my system faster.' She slowly backed out through the kitchen door into the hallway.

Jardine slammed the door shut. 'Tell me what to do,' he pleaded with her.

'First of all, take the rings off my fingers,' Christine said. 'Then take your tie off and wrap it around my arm, four or five inches above the wound.'

Jardine did as he was told, wrenching off his tie and winding it around her arm.

'Now tie it as tight as you can,' Christine instructed. 'Like a tourniquet. It will give me some extra time — a half-hour at least.'

Jardine pulled the tie until it bit into the soft flesh of her arm, tying it off with a double knot. 'Now what?'

'Now you'll have to drive me to Casco, and then on to the hospital,' Christine said.

Jardine didn't understand. 'Why Casco? Why don't I just take you straight to hospital?'

'You can pick up the anti-venom there — it will save time,' Christine told him. 'You'll need me there to give the security man the okay. Now, help me to the car — but try not to move my arm any more than you have to.'

Jardine got her into the car, tucking her injured arm under the seat belt to help keep it immobilised. Setting the siren and light, he pulled away from the kerb as gently as possible, quickly accelerating to full speed. The traffic lights were red at the first intersection. Jardine jabbed his hand on the horn and kept it there, shooting the lights and narrowly missing a group of youths in a red Cortina whose car stereo had been turned up so high that it drowned out everything else.

Christine remained icily calm throughout. In fact, to an observer, it would have seemed that Jardine was the one in trouble.

'When we get to the lab, you'll have to go to the fridge where the anti-venoms are kept,' Christine was saying. 'You remember I showed you once.'

Jardine nodded. 'I remember.'

'You'll find that all the anti-venoms are marked with a code number,' Christine went on. 'Some of them are polyspecific — which means that they can be used to treat bites from a number of different snakes. The one which bit me was a Saw-Scaled viper — I think it's number seven, but you'd better check the list on the inside of the fridge door.'

Jardine muttered to himself, memorising Christine's instructions. 'Saw-Scaled viper, number seven.' He took a right turn, keeping his eyes firmly on the road ahead as he spoke to her again. 'Christine, do you have any idea who would want to do this to you.'

'None at all. It doesn't make any sense at all.'

Jardine glanced anxiously at the car clock. 'How much time do we have?'

Christine looked at it too. They had been in the car for about three minutes, and she had been bitten about six minutes before that. Given the precautions she had taken, and a bit of luck, there seemed no immediate need to panic.

'It'll take you about ten minutes to get to the lab, find the anti-venom and get it back to the car. Provided you can get me to the hospital within quarter of an hour, I should be all right.'

Jardine thumbed the police radio, putting out a call for a police car to meet them at the Casco building. 'That should save us another couple of minutes,' he said. He was calming down himself now. Christine's incredible ability to keep cool had not only impressed, it had affected him. He felt an enormous sense of respect for her. 'You're an incredibly brave girl, Christine — do you know that?'

She managed a weak little laugh. 'That's all *you* know, Michael Jardine. Actually, I'm scared stiff.'

Jardine turned into the industrial estate which housed the Casco complex.

'Go round to the back entrance,' Christine suggested. 'There'll be a security guard on duty and there's a quick way up the back stairs to the lab.'

'Which way?' Jardine wanted to know. He was a little disorientated in the maze of factories and small business units. He had only driven to the Casco building in the daytime, and then to the front of the main complex.

'About half a mile further up this avenue you'll see a small access road on your right,' Christine told him. 'Turn off there and then take the second left. I'll tell you when we're there.'

Jardine reached for the radio again. 'Is that car on its way yet?' he asked urgently.

The controller's voice was friendly, almost jovial. She had no idea of the emergency. 'You're in luck,' came the reply. 'There was a car patrolling that industrial estate when you called in. It'll probably be there before you are.'

'Fine. Tell the driver to meet us at the back entrance — I repeat, the back entrance. Have you go that?'

'Affirmative.' The controller had noticed the urgency in Jardine's tone and had started to realise that the situation was serious. 'Do you need any further back-up?'

'No thanks,' Jardine said. He went to switch off the radio then had a second thought. 'Look, tell the driver that there is a girl in my car who needs to get to hospital as quickly as possible. She's been bitten by a venomous snake. Tell him to take my car and drive her there. He must tell the doctors that I'm on my way with the antidote. I'll use the police car.'

They were coming up to a right-hand turning. Jardine glanced aside at Christine to check that it was the right one. She was lolling back in the seat, her eyes only half-open. Her face looked feverish and sweaty.

'Christine — are you all right?' Jardine hissed anxiously.

Her mouth opened weakly. She managed to speak, but her voice was little more than a whisper. 'Going . . . to pass out . . . any minute,' she informed him. 'Remember — Saw-Scaled viper . . . number . . .'

Christine's eyes fluttered a couple of times and then closed. Jardine forced himself to remain calm. 'Yes, number seven, Christine. I remember,' he whispered, even though she could no longer hear him.

He turned off the main avenue into a network of small access roads and loading bays. There were virtually no street lights. For a moment he started to panic, fearing that he would get lost. Then, ahead of him, he saw the flashing blue light of a waiting police car and breathed a sigh of relief.

Jardine slowed the car to a stop behind the police car. The driver was already out waiting for him.

'I raised the security guard, sir. He's unlocked the back entrance and he's waiting to take you up to the lab.'

Jardine jumped out of the car. 'Right — you've got your instructions. Now get going,' he snapped.

He headed for the back of the Casco building at a run as the police constable climbed into his car and drove off.

Jardine was reaching for his ID card as he approached the security guard, waiting anxiously by the open doorway. The guard touched him lightly on the sleeve. 'No need, sir. I know Miss Gray. Follow me, please.' He turned, leading the way to a flight of bare concrete stairs and bounding up them two at a time.

Grateful for even a few extra seconds, Jardine followed his lead. Thoughtfully, the guard had also tripped the emergency lights, so the building was fully illuminated. Jardine reached the second-floor level and ran through the fire door which the guard held open for him.

'First corridor on the left, sir ... you know the toxinology lab I take it?'

Too out of breath to shout a confirmation, Jardine merely nodded and kept running.

He found the fridge and opened it. As Christine had said, there was a list of all the anti-venoms and their code numbers on the inside of the door. Jardine checked it carefully, confirming number seven as the correct antidote for the venom of the Saw-Scaled viper. Thankfully, the white plastic containers were all clearly marked with large red numbers. Jardine selected a phial of number seven and slipped it into his pocket. He took a precious couple of seconds off to check his watch. There were now just twelve minutes left of Christine's estimated safety time.

Jardine broke into a run again, heading back to the stairs. Given luck, and a bit of fast driving, he could make the hospital in ten.

Chapter Seventeen

Taggart and DC Reid were waiting in the street outside Christine Gray's flat as Jardine arrived straight from the hospital.

Taggart nodded grimly by way of greeting. 'How is she?'

Jardine looked despondent. 'She's in the intensive care unit. They've administered the anti-venom and they're keeping her on life support until she gets a little stronger. There's a good chance of recovery, they say.'

'Well, then you've done everything you can,' Taggart said, smiling reassuringly. 'Come on, Michael – don't take it so personally.'

Jardine would not be consoled. He kicked out at a nearby street lamp in impotent anger. 'Damn it – I should have realised,' he spat out, venting the anger he felt with himself. 'I just wasn't using my brain. The heating was turned up full as we walked into flat. Christine even commented on it – said it shouldn't have been turned up so high. I'm supposed to be a detective, for Christ's sake. I'm supposed to be trained to react to things like that.'

Taggart let him blow off steam for a while, understanding the sense of frustration and self-anger. He remembered the many times he had tortured himself with similar worries and self-recriminations. If only . . . if only I'd realised, if only I'd acted sooner, if only I'd listened to that inner voice. The list was endless. The unnecessary victims a tragedy. It was one of the worst aspects of the job, made even more depressing by the fact that it was also inevitable.

'Calm yourself, Michael,' Taggart said finally, when Jardine's explosion of anger had simmered down to a sullen rage. 'Now, does she have any idea why someone should want to kill her? Is there anyone who could possibly profit from her death?'

Jardine was glad of the chance to get back on the job. He shook his head slowly. 'I asked her, but she can't think of any reason. But it has to be connected with Dr Nielson in some way. She spent most of the day being debriefed on his research by Derek Amlot and Casco's research director, Maureen MacDonald. She was going to tell me all about it tonight.'

Taggart mulled over this information thoughtfully. The facts would imply a connection, certainly – but then nothing about the whole case seemed to follow any logical pattern.

Jackie Reid interrupted his reveries with the announcement of Sullivan's arrival. Cheerful as ever, he strolled up carrying his inevitable cloth bag and tongs.

He grinned at Taggart. 'What have you got for me this time? Another kitten? Or maybe a rampant tortoise?'

Taggart glared at him warningly. Sullivan read the signs and wiped the grin from his face.

'It's a Saw-Scaled viper. In the kitchen,' Jardine told him flatly.

Sullivan's face darkened. 'Ugh, aggressive little things. Kill more people than any other snake I know.'

He turned in the gate and began to stroll up the path. Jackie Reid looked up at Taggart. 'Cheery soul, isn't he?'

Taggart grunted, watched Sullivan disappear inside the house and leaned back against the gatepost to wait.

He was in the flat for a good ten minutes. When he re-emerged, Sullivan was holding the bulging cloth bag at a distance from his body. 'Have to treat these little beauties with a bit of respect,' he announced. 'Take a bit of extra time and care.' He nodded over his shoulder. 'You can go in now.'

'Could there be any others?' Taggart asked.

Sullivan shrugged carelessly. 'Didn't see any.'

'Thanks a lot for the extra time and care,' Taggart muttered sarcastically. It was not exactly the positive assurance he had been seeking.

Sullivan hefted the cloth bag in the air. 'Well, I'll keep this one at the zoo with the others — until you let me know what you want to do with them.'

Taggart suddenly remembered that there *were* others — and some still unaccounted for. 'How long are you attached to Glasgow Zoo for?' asked Taggart.

'I was planning to go back south in the next couple of days,' the man said. 'But I'll stay on a bit longer if you want me to.'

Taggart nodded. 'That might be a good idea. I'd appreciate it.' He followed Sullivan to his van, where he gently laid the bagged snake in a metal cage. 'You seem to handle these things without fear,' he observed, impressed despite himself.

Sullivan gave a sardonic laugh. 'Oh no, you've got to have fear,' he said. He pointed to his scarred face. 'See that? That was a Puff Adder.' He rolled up his sleeve, to reveal a large strip of blackened, wrinkled skin. 'And an Eastern Diamond rattlesnake did that when I wasn't being as careful as I should have.' He laughed again. 'No — man learned his fear of snakes for a good reason. They have been around on this planet for a lot longer than we have.' He closed the back of the van and locked it. 'Well, I'll probably be seeing you again,' he said, moving to the driver's door and opening it.

'I hope not,' Taggart said — although there was a nagging feeling in his gut that he would be proved wrong.

Sullivan drove off, whistling to himself cheerfully. Taggart returned to Jardine and DC Reid, who had made no attempt to enter the flat.

'Well, shall we go in?' he asked, as though he was inviting them in to a vicar's tea-party. The expert had just told him that it was right to have fear. In Taggart's book, that made it acceptable.

'Whoever did it must have known her domestic routine, sir,' Jackie Reid observed as she entered the hall.

Taggart raised one eyebrow quizzically. 'How so?'

'Well, for a start, they knew that she would come in and feed the dog and they knew the dog food was kept in the larder. That would imply at least casual acquaintance with the premises and her way of life, wouldn't you say?'

Taggart nodded thoughtfully. 'Good thinking,' he said. He was impressed.

Jardine came into the kitchen waving an envelope in his hand. 'I think you ought to take a look at this, sir. I found it in Christine's coat pocket.'

'What is it?' Taggart asked, taking the envelope.

'It's a letter of resignation,' Jardine said. 'Interesting, don't you think? Christine Gray is attacked by a venomous snake on the very day she announced her intention to leave Casco — just like Dr Nielson.'

Taggart examined the envelope, noting that it had been opened. He pulled the letter out and scanned through it. 'It was like this . . . opened . . . when you found it?'

Jardine nodded. 'Which suggests that somebody had read it.'

'And acted on it?' Taggart mused. 'It would seem that people have a hard time getting away from Casco Pharmaceuticals. I would be very interested to know if our Mr Amlot had actually read this letter.'

'Why don't we ask him, sir?' Jackie Reid suggested.

Taggart nodded. 'Good idea.' He turned to Jardine. 'Get on to his home number. If he's not there, ask his wife where he is. And if she doesn't know, try that hotel where Mrs Nielson is staying.'

'Can I go with him, sir?' Jackie Reid asked. 'I'd rather like to see that man sweat a little.'

'Aye.' Taggart sucked at his teeth. 'Two of you will put a bit more pressure on him — perhaps make him let something slip.'

'Do you really think he could have murdered Nielson just to prevent him leaving, sir?' Jardine asked. 'Is he a real suspect?'

Taggart shrugged hopelessly. 'I don't know, Michael — but right now, what else have we got?'

Jackie Reid got her wish. Derek Amlot was already sweating profusely when she and Jardine tracked him down at his squash club. Already well beaten by a younger, and much fitter partner, he smashed the ball ineffectually to the side wall as he caught sight of the pair of them regarding him from the inspection gallery above the court.

'Had enough, Derek?' his partner asked, grinning.

Amlot nodded up at the gallery. 'I have visitors.' Letting his racquet droop, he strode out of the court into the changing-rooms.

He was stripped to the waist and towelling the sweat from his body when Jackie Reid led the way into the changing-room. Amlot gave her a superior, even taunting, look. 'Ah, the young police-woman who enters bedrooms without knocking. I won't be embarrassing you, then?'

Jackie returned his gaze with a cool, level stare. 'Not in the slightest,' she said dismissively, noting with some satisfaction that he seemed to be disappointed.

Jardine caught his eye and held it. 'Christine Gray is in hospital. Someone tried to kill her tonight.'

Jardine had been looking for the faintest flicker of reaction, but found none. Amlot received the news as a cold statement of fact, which apparently triggered no personal feelings whatsoever. Jardine wondered, briefly, what romantic attraction he had for Morag Nielson. Emotionally, Derek Amlot seemed to be a cold fish.

'I'm sorry to hear that,' was all that Amlot said, the words no more than perfunctory.

'I believe she spent most of the day with you and Dr MacDonald, going through Dr Nielson's recent work?'

Amlot nodded. 'That's right. And very helpful she was, too. But

I can't see how this should concern me outside of office hours. Couldn't you wait until the morning?'

Jardine produced Christine's letter from his pocket. 'You know what this is, I suppose?'

Amlot took the letter and glanced at it for no more than a second. 'Yes, it's a letter of resignation. I read it. I told her not to be so stupid and to go home and think it over.'

'Someone didn't give her the chance,' Jardine said pointedly. 'Odd, isn't it, how nasty things happen to people who try to leave your company.'

Amlot's eyes narrowed. 'Are you accusing me of something?' he demanded. 'In which case we should terminate this conversation now, until I have had a chance to consult with my solicitor.'

Jardine avoided the direct confrontation. 'How valuable was Christine Gray's research?' he asked.

Amlot paused, analysing the situation coldly. Finally, he accepted that the change of tack was a back-down on Jardine's part and seemed to relax again. 'You really are getting quite paranoid, do you know that? Do you seriously suppose that just because our employees want to move on that we take out some sort of a contract on their lives?' Amlot's eyes bored into Jardine's for a moment, finally identifying the possibility that he was, indeed, considering it seriously. 'Look, she was a junior research assistant, that's all. She was working on a project, yes — but strictly second-level stuff.'

'That's not quite what I understood from Miss Gray,' Jardine said. 'She believed that the potential value of her research was very high indeed.'

Amlot shrugged it off dismissively. 'Yes, well — scientists do like to feel important, don't they?'

'And Dr Nielson's work? Was that of minor importance?' Jackie Reid put in.

Amlot ignored her, concentrating on Jardine. 'Look, if you want to find out who tried to kill Christine. I suggest you look into her personal life. A jealous boyfriend, perhaps. I think she liked her men-friends, if you know what I mean.'

'The same jealous boyfriend who also killed Dr Nielson?'

Jardine asked coldly. 'Someone put another venomous snake in her flat. One of the snakes taken from your lab.'

Amlot reacted for the first time. Jardine noted the look of worry which flickered across his face. 'Then I suggest you start looking for a maniac,' Amlot said. 'Because only a maniac would do something like that.'

He glanced sideways as the changing-room door swung open. Morag Nielson walked in, saw the two detectives and stopped in her tracks, uncertainly.

'Excuse me,' Amlot muttered to Jardine. With an angry look on his face he strode over to Morag and grasped her by the arm, marching her back outside to the lobby.

'Why have you come here?' he hissed angrily. 'Are you deliberately trying to give these bloody detectives more excuse to hound me?'

Morag shrugged his hand away from her arm. She was angry too. 'I wanted to talk to you. I've been phoning your secretary all day but she kept saying that you were busy.'

'I was,' Amlot snapped. He heard the changing-room door sigh open behind him. 'Damn — here come those bloody police again.' He pushed Morag away from him roughly. 'Go and wait for me in the bar. I'll come as soon as I can get rid of them.'

He turned to face Jardine and DC Reid again, resuming his bland, outwardly calm expression.

'Now, if you've quite finished, I would like to enjoy what's left of my leisure,' he said. 'I've had an extremely busy day, and I could do without these intrusions into my social life.'

Jardine refused to give the man the satisfaction of thinking he had terminated the interview. 'We were just leaving, Mr Amlot,' he said. 'We'll be in touch if there's anything else we want to know.'

Amlot watched them depart with a vaguely worried look on his face. Things were getting far too claustrophobic for his liking — as though the walls were closing in around him. And now Morag appeared to be getting increasingly possessive. It really was too much. Amlot disliked having any part of his life put in the spotlight. There was too much at risk, too much to lose. He returned to the changing-room to finish dressing, racking his brains for a good and convincing excuse for getting rid of Morag Nielson.

Taggart took a last look around Christine's flat, satisfying himself that the fingerprint boys had covered everything — particularly the kitchen area and around the central heating control console.

Not that he expected it to yield much, he reminded himself pessimistically. A similar sweep in Nielson's house had turned up nothing other than the fact that the intruder had probably been wearing leather gloves. Sighing, Taggart left them to it, after giving explicit instructions that he wanted the results on McVitie's desk first thing in the morning.

He returned to his car, feeling at something of a loose end. He knew that he ought to go home, yet something inside was urging him that there were more questions to be asked, so many answers to find. Taggart recognised the feeling. He knew it only too well. It meant that the case was getting through to him on a personal level. Despite all the years, all the cases, and all the many times he had reminded himself that a policeman needed a professional detachment — it still happened, all too frequently.

He started the car and drove off. It came as almost a surprise to him to realise that he was not heading home at all, but for Annie Gilmour's house.

The downstairs lights were still on. Taggart walked up the front drive and pressed the bell. Annie answered almost immediately.

'I know it's late, Annie,' Taggart apologised. 'But could I come in for a minute?'

'Of course, Jim.' Annie held back the door, welcoming him into the house.

He strolled straight through into the front room and seated himself.

'A drink, Jim? You look as though you could do with one,' Annie offered. Without waiting for an answer, she crossed to the sideboard and poured him out a measure of whisky.

Taggart accepted the drink gratefully, waiting until Annie had poured one for herself and seated herself opposite him.

'I just wondered — whether you'd had any more thoughts about that pharmaceutical company,' Taggart said finally. Even as he spoke, he realised that he was probably poking at a dead-end, but he knew he had to try.

Annie shook her head. 'I've racked my brains, Jim. Janet never said anything about a company called Casco — I'm sure.'

Taggart sighed. It was nothing less than he had expected. He sipped at his drink for a while. 'There has to be a connection, Annie — there just has to be. Someone didn't want her identified, and that someone had a very strong connection to Casco Pharmaceuticals. There's a link in here somewhere, if only we could find it.'

Annie could sense his frustration, almost desperation. She smiled gently. 'It's not important. Not any more,' she said, strangely. 'Janet's back with us now — that's all that matters.'

Taggart looked at her with a puzzled expression on his face. Something was just starting to dawn on him — something which had never crossed his mind before. 'You don't really want to know who killed her, do you?' he muttered.

Annie shrugged faintly. 'All these years, Jim. These four long years, all I wanted was to know where she was, why she went away. I know that now. It's enough.'

Taggart looked into her eyes for a while, understanding and not understanding at the same time.

'Did you ask that young man . . . about the sculpture?' Annie asked, at length.

Taggart shook his head, wearily. 'I'm sorry, Annie. I forgot. I'll do it tomorrow, I promise.'

Annie's face had a dreamy, almost contented look on it. 'That face . . . so beautiful. So . . . vibrant. It's as though he did it from life,' she murmured softly.

Taggart finished his whisky and pushed himself up out of the chair. There was nothing more for him here, he realised. For Annie, all the loose ends had been tied up; the jigsaw puzzle was completed. If only his own job could be so simple. 'Thanks for the drink, Annie,' he said. 'And I'll ask about the bust, I promise.'

He made his own way to the door, letting himself out into the cold silence of the night.

A high-pitched electronic alarm shrilled from the monitor above Christine Gray's hospital bed. A nurse rushed into the IC unit, took one look at the feverish, convulsing body in the bed and hurried out again, searching for the doctor. The girl was having some sort of allergic reaction — possibly to the anti-venom injection.

It did not look good.

Chapter Eighteen

Sullivan strolled aimlessly through the reptile house of Glasgow Zoo, feeling more than a little frustrated. A whole day to kill, and nothing of any importance to do. It was annoying. Had he been able to follow his original plans, he would be well on his way back to Chester now, away from Glasgow and all its old and painful memories.

There had been a girl once, in this cold and lonely city. A young, beautiful girl, who had told him that she loved him. But that was before the accident, the careless oversight in handling a Puff Adder that had allowed it to sink its ugly fangs into his face and pump its vicious poison into his blood.

Sullivan raised his hand to his cheek, fingering the scarred tissue absently and remembering. How the plastic surgeons had warned him that he would bear the marks for life, how people might find his once-handsome face repulsive, even frightening.

... And the look in her eyes when she had first seen the gruesome results. The fear, in her, that she would never again be able to tell him that she loved him without betraying herself in a lie.

And now he was stuck in this city which had let him down so badly. Stuck because he had allowed Taggart to manoeuvre him into staying on. Sullivan cursed himself for being Mr Nice Guy again. Sometimes the cheerful, easy-going image got hard to maintain.

He passed Colin Murphy, just launching into his routine with a party of schoolchildren. Sullivan leaned back against a wall, watching the young man and despising him for turning snakes into a form of entertainment.

Murphy had a young constrictor coiled around his shoulders, its head resting on the back of the young man's hand. 'Now, can any of you children tell me what kind of snake this is?' Murphy asked, geeing up his young audience to a pitch of excitement.

'It's a python, mister,' one young lad said proudly, eager to show off his knowledge to his peers.

Murphy turned to the child with a playful gleam in his eyes. 'Wrong,' he announced. 'It's a python.' As ever, he paused to let the children enjoy a laugh at the expense of the confused boy. 'Actually, it's a very young python and he's very tame. I think! Now — can any of you tell me how pythons kill their prey?'

This time the children were less eager to respond. Finally, the urge to show off overcame the fear of being shown up, and a young girl answered. 'They crush it,' she volunteered.

'Right,' Murphy exclaimed. He edged the python upwards with his hand, so that it started to shift its coils around his neck. 'So the very last thing you want to do is to let a python coil itself around your neck.' He pretended to suddenly notice that his python was doing exactly that and feigned terror. 'Oh, help, help!'

The children gasped in fear, sucked into the charade. Murphy grinned, uncoiled the snake and held it out towards them, showing how harmless it really was. 'Now, who would like to touch him? He's really very friendly, I promise.'

As the children pushed forward in a mass, Sullivan shrugged himself away from the wall. He had seen enough of the stupid clowning. Any more would only upset him. Snakes were not playthings, objects to be used as cheap entertainment. They were fascinating, but deadly, and they commanded respect.

Sullivan walked towards the breeding room, fishing his key out of his pocket. The area was closed to the public now, while serving as temporary accommodation for the recovered Casco reptiles. He passed a young woman seated on a portable chair with a small easel, busily sketching a tank of lizards.

Probably a young art student, Sullivan thought. The girl was blonde, and very attractive. She reminded him of that other girl, so many years ago. He stopped beside her, looking down and admiring her work.

The girl looked up at him, a smile already forming on her face. Then her eyes took in his scarred face, and the smile died before it was fully born. Sullivan recognised that look, and it tore at his gut. Moving away abruptly, he let himself into the breeding room and looked around at the glass tanks.

He crossed to the nearest tank where the Saw-Scaled viper which had bitten Christine Gray lay quiet and unmoving. It uncoiled slowly, sensing his approach, hissing warningly.

Sullivan reached out and touched the side of the tank. The viper struck like lightning, its fangs clicking against the glass.

Sullivan smiled to himself. You knew where you were with snakes. There was no pretence, no lies. They just hated you, and wanted to kill you, and that was all there was to it.

Jardine strode purposefully through the hospital towards the intensive care unit, closely followed by Jackie Reid, who had come along to keep him company more than anything else. He was still very upset, continuing to blame himself for Christine's condition.

Jackie stayed back as Jardine sought out the young doctor handling Christine's case, and flashed his ID card. 'Christine Gray, doctor. How is she?'

Dr Scott's face was set in a stern, professional mask, giving little away. 'She's weak — much weaker than we would like,' he admitted. 'She suffered a severe allergic reaction to the anti-venom last night.' He broke off, seeing the concern on Jardine's face. 'Oh, it's not uncommon,' he hastened to reassure Jardine. 'But we had to administer adrenalin and antihistamines, and there can be further complications.'

'Can I see her?' Jardine asked.

Dr Scott thought for a moment, shaking his head uncertainly. 'She's certainly not up to questioning, that's for sure.' He paused, his tone becoming more gentle. 'You're the young man who was with her last night, aren't you?'

Jardine nodded. 'This isn't police business. I'd just like to see her. I'm a friend.'

Scott seemed to concede against his better judgement. 'Just a few moments, then. But don't try to get her to talk.'

Jardine nodded understandingly. 'Thanks,' he said simply. He pushed open the swing doors of the IC unit and walked in.

He pulled up a chair beside her bed and sat down, regarding her fondly. Even now, her eyes sunken and her face the colour of raw clay, she was still beautiful. A fresh wave of regret tore at him, for the chance missed and the unforgivable lapse in his professional judgement.

Christine's eyes fluttered weakly as she recognised him. Her mouth opened to speak, but Jardine laid a finger across her lips, stilling them.

'Shussh,' he murmured. 'Don't try to talk. Everything is going to be all right.'

He sat in silence for several minutes, just looking at her and listening to the faint bleep of the monitor above her bed.

'I'm looking after your dog,' he told her after a while. 'He's fine, but I think he's missing you a little.'

Christine's eyes flickered with gratitude.

'We're going to get the crazy bastard who did this to you,' Jardine promised. He noticed that her brow was beaded with perspiration and extracted a tissue from a box on the bedside table. He bent over her, mopping her brow gently.

There was something in the corner of her eye. Jardine took a fresh tissue, screwed it into a thin spill and dabbed gently at the small, dark speck. A slight shiver of apprehension ran through him as the object burst, revealing itself as a small globule of blood which quickly soaked into the tissue. Even as it was absorbed, another larger bubble of red prickled out in its place.

With growing alarm, Jardine looked at her other eye. It, too, was beginning to seep blood. Suddenly, Christine's body gave a small, convulsive jerk. Her head lolled sideways, her mouth dropping open. Jardine's guts knotted as a thin stream of gore trickled out over her lips and ran down her chin on to the pillow.

Jardine jumped to his feet, panicking. He rushed through the door, screaming for the doctor. 'She's bleeding . . . it's coming out of her eyes and her mouth.'

Dr Scott and a nurse ran past him and hurried into the IC ward. Jardine turned to follow them, but his way was barred by an orderly who had appeared from nowhere to guard the doors. Jackie Reid stepped up behind him, laying her hand gently on his shoulder. 'It's probably nothing, Michael,' she whispered, attempting to comfort him.

Jardine whirled on her, an innocent victim upon which to vent his anger and frustration. 'She's bleeding internally. It's coming out of her eyes, for God's sake!'

Jackie let his rage wash over her, sharing his anguish. 'It's not your fault,' she told him, knowing that he wasn't listening.

Jardine bit at his bottom lip savagely. 'If only I'd been a few seconds quicker. If I'd just been on the ball, which I wasn't.'

Jackie threw her arms around him. 'No one can blame you, Michael. So you mustn't blame yourself.'

Jardine shrugged her off, feeling unclean like a leper. 'The central heating was turned up full in her flat. Just like it was in Dr Nielson's. I should have realised. I should have known.'

He walked away, quickly, needing to be on his own and not wishing Jackie to see the tears which were welling in his eyes.

Chapter Nineteen

Angus Mackay looked too damned pleased with himself, Amlot thought as the scientist breezed into his office. He was used to the man's usual ebullience, even arrogance, but there was something especially smug about his expression this morning which portended problems.

'Well, what is this matter which you consider so urgent?' Amlot asked, as Mackay seated himself without being asked. He wondered if the confounded man was trying to rile him deliberately. He had already had the cheek to book his own appointment directly with Amlot's personal secretary, instead of going through the usual departmental channels.

Mackay crossed his legs, lolling back in the chair. 'Fact is, I've been offered another job,' he announced proudly. 'Strangely enough, through the same head-hunting agency which approached Doug Nielson.'

Amlot tried to assimilate the bombshell without over-reacting. He failed. The traumatic events of the past few days had taken their toll on his normal self-control, leaving him rattled and on edge. His face fell. 'My God, Angus — this is getting to be a bloody epidemic,' he blurted out. 'First Nielson, then Christine — and now you. What is this — lemming-time for Casco employees?'

Mackay retained his smug expression. 'Well, I hope I don't meet with the same fate,' he said. With no attempt at modesty, he added: 'Of course, it was bound to happen sooner or later, Derek. I am one of the five top men in my field, after all.'

Amlot conceded the point. In actual fact, he was surprised that it hadn't happened before. 'Who?' he asked.

Mackay fiddled with his bow-tie. 'Thorne Camfield, actually. Not the greatest of career moves, I admit — but I'm told they have already earmarked a further two and a half million for research in the current financial year.'

'How much?' was Amlot's next question.

Mackay had been waiting for it. He grinned expansively, as if enjoying some huge joke. 'Oh, about twelve thousand more than you're about to offer me now.'

Amlot was not amused. 'At least credit me with some generosity.' He paused, thinking of something else which might appeal to Mackay's vastly over-inflated ego. 'Of course, there's the scientific convention in California coming up in March. What would you say to spending a month over there as our top representative? All expenses paid, of course.'

Mackay considered. He was tempted, but it didn't seem a good ploy to appear too impressed. 'That's extremely kind of you, Derek — but I have been here rather a long time, and I do sometimes feel that the grass is reaching my ears.'

Amlot detected the first, faint signs of vacillation. 'Look, why don't we go out to dinner tonight, discuss this like gentlemen over a few bottles of good wine?' He reached for his intercom. 'Any place in particular?' he asked Mackay before pressing the button.

Mackay thought for a couple of seconds. 'Well, I did hear about a very good new French restaurant which has just opened uptown,' he murmured. 'Frightfully expensive, of course . . .'

Amlot fingered the intercom button. 'Oh, Caroline. Could you book a table at La Pigalle for Dr Mackay and myself this evening?'

His secretary was the epitome of efficiency. 'I'll do it straight-away,' she said briskly. 'Oh, and by the way — Chief Inspector Taggart is here. He wants to see Dr MacDonald. I thought you'd want to know.'

'Yes, thanks, Caroline.' Amlot flicked off the intercom, the faintest trace of a frown creasing his forehead.

Mackay seized on it with undisguised glee. 'Perhaps I should ask him for round-the-clock protection while he's here. Casco employees seem to be something of an endangered species just lately.'

Amlot forced himself to smile. 'Oh, I don't think that's really necessary, Angus,' he said in a friendly tone, whilst loathing the flamboyant little man. 'Well, we'll continue this discussion to-night, then. Over dinner.'

Mackay got to his feet, unable to resist one last little jibe. 'I am glad you said dinner, Derek. If you'd invited me out for a bite, I might have been very suspicious.'

Amlot glared after him as he left, wondering if he had been too impulsive in promising him inducements to stay on. Unlike Nielson, Angus Mackay was comparatively expendable. His work, though of value in terms of prestige and day-to-day turnover, was basically routine. Perhaps, after all, he reflected, it might not be such a bad thing if Angus Mackay were to disappear from Casco — one way or another.

He thumbed his intercom, calling Maureen MacDonald's office. 'Oh, Maureen. Can you prepare a quick update on Angus Mackay's current projects? He's been got at by the Management Quest outfit, and he's threatening to quit. I need to know how much we stand to lose if we let him go.' Amlot suddenly remembered Taggart. 'Oh, yes — and Taggart is on his way up to see you. You will be discreet, won't you? We really can't afford to let it become public knowledge how much we had riding on Nielson's research work.'

There was a momentary pause as Maureen MacDonald inter-preted the full significance of her employer's apparently casual comments.

'I understand, Derek,' she said finally, and snapped off her intercom at the precise second that Taggart knocked on her office door. 'Come,' she called imperiously.

Taggart stepped in, sweeping the luxuriously appointed office with a critical eye. 'Must be a lot of money in the chemicals business,' he observed.

Maureen smiled disarmingly, motioning him to a chair. 'There's a lot of money in cosmetics, Chief Inspector — and that's exactly what this is. Unfortunately, Casco never got into the powders and perfumes market. We're at the sharp end of serious scientific research.'

Taggart seated himself. 'I take it you've heard about Christine Gray?'

Maureen nodded. 'Yes, and I'm both shocked and saddened by it,' she said, with obvious sincerity. 'Who would want to do such a thing?'

'Obviously, the same someone who wanted to do it to Dr Nielson,' Taggart muttered, studying the woman's eyes for a reaction.

There was none. 'So a connection between the two doesn't surprise you?' Taggart said.

Maureen's eyebrows lifted fractionally. 'You're asking my opinion, Chief Inspector? I'm flattered.' She thought carefully for a while. 'No, surprise is not the word. It's quite obvious that there must *be* a connection, but I find it totally baffling.'

Taggart changed tack. 'I understand that Christine Gray spent several hours with you and Derek Amlot yesterday. What was the purpose of that meeting, exactly?'

'To find out what Dr Nielson was working on when he died,' Maureen answered simply. 'Only Christine would have had any real understanding of his latest notes and records.'

Taggart looked surprised. 'But you're the research director. Didn't *you* know?'

Maureen smiled. 'You obviously don't understand the workings of the scientific mind, Chief Inspector. Scientific research isn't like work in an office or a factory, where the boss knows exactly what every worker is doing and what gets produced at the end of the day. Research consultants are the boffins in this business, and up to a point they're a law unto themselves. They usually have what's called a roving brief to carry out research in what could be a fairly large field. Sometimes no one knows quite what they're up to.'

Taggart nodded. 'Sounds like a good job,' he muttered. 'So what kind of research was Dr Nielson concerned with?'

Maureen was remembering Amlot's warning, but there did not seem any point in trying to conceal the basic facts. 'Molecular genetics, in broad scope. Immunisation, toxin research. More specifically, the use of neurotoxins to try to find a cure for muscular dystrophy.'

Taggart was impressed. 'And all this from snake venom?'

'Natural toxins,' Maureen corrected him gently.

Taggart wasn't really interested in buzz words and euphemisms. Poison was poison. 'Surely a cure for a disease like muscular dystrophy would be worth millions, wouldn't it?'

Maureen repressed a thin smile. For all his bluff outer camouflage, Taggart performed with all the skill and subtlety of a surgeon. She had hardly noticed the scalpel slicing through into the raw meat of the matter. With Amlot's warning in mind, she sought a means to distract him.

Fortuitously, Angus Mackay chose that moment to pass by her office. Maureen saw him through the glass of her office door and caught his eye. Raising her hand, she beckoned him, smiling like a long-lost friend.

Somewhat bemused by this sudden, and extremely uncharacteristic, show of camaraderie, Mackay stopped in his tracks, stepped back and poked his head around the door.

'Congratulations, Angus,' Maureen gushed. 'Derek told me the good news.'

Mackay was, for once, rendered speechless. The most he could manage was a half-grin and a faint nod of his head. He retreated, closing the door behind him and walking away with a puzzled frown on his face.

Maureen returned her attention to Taggart. 'That was Dr

Mackay,' she explained. 'He's another of our research consultants. Into allergies. He's just been poached by the multinational Thorne Camfield. By the same recruitment agency who approached Dr Nielson, believe it or not.'

The mere suggestion of a possible link was enough to interest Taggart and pull him off track. 'This agency – do you get the feeling that they seem to have it in for Casco?' he asked.

Maureen smiled. 'Oh, it happens all the time, in virtually all top management. It's merely that Management Quest specialise in the scientific field, and we just happen to be one of only a handful of the larger research establishments in the Glasgow area. It's certainly not a personal vendetta, I can assure you.'

But Taggart wasn't really listening to her. In the back of his mind he was recalling DC Reid's words when she had made her report earlier that morning. 'Christine Gray is in a bad way, sir. It seems she suffered a severe allergic reaction.'

Taggart leaned forward in his chair, his eyes narrowing. 'You said Mackay specialised in allergies, Dr MacDonald.'

Maureen nodded. 'Yes, he's one of the top men in his field.'

Taggart was well hooked now. 'So, would his work overlap with Dr Nielson's in any way? Could they, for instance, have collaborated on some joint project which you didn't know about?'

Maureen thought about it for a moment, finally shaking her head. 'It's vaguely possible that there might have been one or two small areas in which they could have pooled ideas – but I think the idea of them ever working together is out of the question. They didn't really like each other.'

'Professional jealousy? Or something more personal?' Taggart probed.

Maureen shrugged. 'Just different personality types, that's all.'

Taggart rose from his chair. The interview had given him a couple of possible new leads to follow up on. For now, it would have to do. 'Oh, just one last thing,' he muttered. 'Why is everyone here so guarded about the potential value of Dr Nielson's research?'

Maureen was completely thrown off guard. 'I'm not quite sure what you mean,' she blustered.

Taggart smiled. 'Oh, I think you have a fair idea,' he said. 'Landsberg Chemicals were prepared to invest over a million in new research facilities alone.'

Aware that she had already given herself away, Maureen Mac-Donald saw no point in trying to deny the fact. 'How did you know that?' she asked, puzzled.

Taggart grinned. 'I phoned them this morning. A bit of home-work.' He let himself out of the office, feeling a slight sense of satisfaction at having ruffled the woman's feathers.

Jardine sat halfway up the metal steps of the fire-escape, his head buried in his hands, as Taggart drove into the police station carpark. Taggart walked slowly towards him. 'What's eating you?'

Jardine raised his head, looking down at Taggart with eyes that were dead and empty. 'Christine Gray died half an hour ago,' he said flatly.

Taggart cursed himself for his stupidity. He should have re-alised. He racked his brain desperately for something to say which would put his young colleague at ease, take away some of his terrible sense of guilt. In the end there was only the obvious, and it sounded trite.

'It wasn't your fault, Michael. You have to hold on to that.'

Jardine rose and stepped down the fire-escape. He shuffled his feet against the tarmac of the carpark as if to reassure himself that his feet were on the ground again. 'McVitie wants to see us both,' he announced. 'I was just waiting for you.'

He turned towards the main building. Taggart fell into step beside him, saying nothing. There was nothing he could offer. Jardine had to come to terms with himself in his own time, and in his own way. Just as he himself had done so many times in the past.

'I called you both in because I feel there's a danger of us losing track of the essential nub of this matter,' McVitie said. 'And that is, whoever is doing these killings desperately wants to prevent us from identifying those skulls.'

'I agree, sir,' Taggart said. 'But until the second face is finished, we haven't been able to take that any further.'

McVitie conceded the point. 'Do we have any idea yet how soon that will be?' he asked.

'Carl Young is hoping to complete the second face tomorrow, sir,' Jardine informed him. 'It's just a matter of fine details. Hopefully, we can then get photographs into the late edition of the *Evening Times*.'

'From then on, it'll be up to the public,' Taggart said. 'We need a name to go with that face.'

McVitie nodded thoughtfully. 'So, let's recap,' he suggested. 'What have we actually got to work on at this present time?'

Taggart summed it up for him. 'What we have are three scientists, all dead. Two of them working for the same company and all involved in projects which were potentially valuable. And now there's a third scientist who wants to leave Casco.'

McVitie looked up in surprise. 'A *third*? This is a new development.'

Taggart nodded. 'I only found out a short time ago. A Dr Mackay — approached by the same headhunting agency who tried to get Neilson.'

'We met Mackay, sir. At the party,' Jardine put in. 'Bit of a wag — real boffin type. From what I could gather not much liked by his colleagues.'

'How vital is his work?' McVitie wanted to know.

'I've been into that too, sir,' Taggart said. 'He's apparently regarded as one of the top brains in the country in allergy research.' Taggart paused for effect. 'And Christine Gray died more from an allergic reaction than from the actual effects of the snakebite.'

McVitie frowned. 'Wait a minute. Aren't we getting just a little paranoid, perhaps?'

Taggart regarded him quizzically. 'But can we afford to ignore it, sir?'

'After Christine's death we can't afford to ignore anything,' Jardine said emphatically.

Something in his tone alerted McVitie to a deeper underlying significance. He glanced briefly at Taggart, one eyebrow raised in a silent question.

'He blames himself for Christine Gray's death, sir,' Taggart explained. 'Wrongly, of course – but it's understandable.'

McVitie's face screwed up, assuming a rueful expression. 'Ah, the benefit of hindsight,' he observed. 'I wish we all had it.'

Jardine's face was set. 'It was the benefit of foresight in this case, sir. And I *did* have it.'

McVitie caught the warning look in Taggart's eyes and let the topic drop. 'So we're effectively at a standstill until tomorrow. Is that an accurate assessment of the situation?'

Taggart nodded in confirmation. 'Other than re-cover old ground, sir. Everything hinges on that second face, at the moment. I'm planning to talk to this recruitment agency, but I'm not really sure what I expect it to yield.'

McVitie tidied the notes on his desk, sighing. 'Well, keep me informed, gentlemen.'

It was a clear signal that the meeting was over. Taggart and Jardine backed out of McVitie's office, exchanging a shared glance which summed up the general air of frustration which was affecting everybody.

'We'll get there, Michael,' Taggart muttered, with far more conviction than he actually felt.

Jardine was unconvinced. 'But how many more people have to die before we do?' he muttered bitterly.

Chapter Twenty

It was a crisp, bright morning. Clad in his warm tracksuit, Derek Amlot completed his second jogging circuit of the park and paused to regain his breath, punching the air with his hands. He stopped, glancing at his watch. It was seven forty-five. Just enough time to drive home, take a shower before breakfast and put in an early show at the office.

He began to walk back to the carpark. He was not pleased to find Morag Nielson waiting for him, leaning against the bonnet of his car. He strode up to her angrily. 'What do you think you're doing, following me around like this? I could have had the kids with me.'

Morag was in no mood to be apologetic. 'But you haven't,' she pointed out, rather superfluously. 'I just wasn't prepared to spend another whole day trying to ring you at the office only to be brushed off with excuses by your bloody secretary.' Morag stared him straight in the eyes. 'Why are you trying to avoid me, Derek?'

Amlot glanced away. 'I'm not avoiding you, Morag. I'm a busy man, you know that.'

Morag pouted sulkily, clutching at his arm. 'You always used to be able to find time to spend with me, Derek. And now we can have lots more time together.'

Amlot's face froze. Pulling himself free, he regarded her coldly. 'Just exactly what do you mean by that?'

Morag shrugged. 'Douglas is dead. That changes things. It changes my future . . . and it changes ours.'

Amlot's expression hardened. 'Does it?' he demanded.

'Well, of course it does,' Morag said in a wheedling tone, grasping his arm again. 'I have nothing to hide any more. That must make it easier for us to see each other.'

Amlot was becoming increasingly horrified. He had never had many illusions about Morag Nielson, accepting her as a cold, hard and calculating woman whose only emotional response was in the bedroom. But this new, possessive Morag was a whole new ball-game. It could only spell trouble.

He looked at her with an almost shocked expression on his face. 'You don't even care who killed Douglas, do you?' he said in disbelief. 'Aren't you even curious?'

Morag tossed her pretty head in a dismissive gesture. 'I'd be more interested to find out who tried to kill me,' she said. 'I was in the house that night – the night he died. I went back to collect a few things. I was actually in the bedroom . . .' Morag broke off, giving a little shudder, ' . . . with that, that . . . *creature.*'

Amlot frowned slightly. 'Did you tell the police that?'

Morag shook her head. 'No, of course not. If I'd told them that, they might have thought that we had murdered Douglas together. You know how their minds work.'

'What about your car?' Amlot asked. 'Didn't somebody see it?'

'I parked it a street away,' Morag told him. 'For the very reason that if Douglas came home unexpectedly, I could sneak away without him being any the wiser. Which is exactly what I did.'

Amlot was thoughtful for a few seconds. 'Perhaps you ought to tell the police,' he said eventually. 'There's no way they can connect me. I have a cast-iron alibi.'

He fished in his pocket, pulling out his car keys and thumbing the automatic door lock button. Reaching for the handle he opened the car door.

Morag pulled at his arm more fiercely. 'You can't just drive away from me,' she said, warningly. 'I want to know when I'm going to see you.'

Amlot shrugged her off. He slid into the car, pulling the door shut behind him and activating the central lock. He slipped the keys into the ignition and started the engine.

Morag wrenched vainly at the door handle, her expression turning to one of anger. 'I'm warning you, Derek — don't try to run out on me,' she shouted at him through the glass of the window.

Amlot flicked the electric window release, allowing the glass to slide down just a few inches. He looked at her with a cool, detached expression. 'Look, this has been a hard decision to take, but you're rather forcing my hand,' he said quietly. 'I've been thinking . . . that I ought to spend more time with my family. What with them and the pressures of the job taking up so much of my time, it's getting difficult. It's time to call it a day. Try to understand.'

Morag's face was a mask of incredulous fury. She couldn't bring herself to believe that any man could reject her out of hand. 'Understand?' she spat angrily. 'I understand that you've just been using me. As long as I was useful in helping to keep Douglas at your precious bloody company.'

Amlot sighed. He had hoped to avoid this final confrontation, but Morag had left him no choice. All he could hope for now was the chance to get away with some remaining vestige of dignity. 'That's nonsense and you know it,' he said, in the same calm and quiet voice. 'I'm sorry, Morag.'

Morag kicked the side of the car in fury, her voice rising to a near-hysterical scream. 'What are you leaving me with? Absolutely nothing!'

Amlot let in the clutch and slid the car into gear. 'The big difference between us is that Douglas never meant a damned thing to you, other than as a meal ticket. My family, on the other hand, mean a great deal to me, and I'm not prepared to see them suffer.'

Amlot wound up the window. He let out the clutch. The car started to move forward, with Morag still desperately trying to wrench open the door. Amlot accelerated, pulling away from her and eventually leaving her standing helplessly alone.

Morag stared at the back of the disappearing car, her normally beautiful face screwed into an angry mask of hatred. 'You bastard,' she screamed after it. 'I'll kill you, you bastard!'

She continued to scream and rant until the car reached the park gates and turned out on to the main road. Then she sat down on the gravel of the carpark and tried to cry.

The release of tears would not come. There was only a cold and furious anger, and the burning need for revenge. Morag rose to her feet and walked slowly towards her own car. Derek Amlot would pay dearly for spurning her, she told herself.

Morag drove around aimlessly for nearly an hour, scheming and plotting. Finally, she drove to Maryhill Police Station.

'I'm Mrs Nielson. I'd like to speak with Detective Chief Inspector Taggart,' she told the young woman constable on desk duty.

The girl consulted her day book and duty roster. 'Sorry, but he's out at the moment,' she said. 'Is there anyone else who can help you?'

Morag thought for a second. She had geared herself up for this and wasn't prepared to let it see the cold light of rationality. 'His young colleague,' she blurted out impulsively. 'The one who interviewed me earlier . . . about my husband's murder.'

'You mean Detective Sergeant Jardine?' the constable said.

Morag nodded. 'Yes — can I speak to him, please?'

WPC Gillis picked up the phone and punched out Jardine's extension number. Jackie Reid answered.

'There's a Mrs Nielson here to see Jardine,' Gillis said. 'Shall I show her into an interview room?'

Jackie glanced across at Jardine, who was seated at his desk doodling on pieces of scrap paper and still moping. 'We'll be right out,' she said without bothering to consult him. Right now, work was the one thing which he needed to occupy his mind.

She hung up the phone and called over. 'Mrs Nielson's here. She wants to talk to us,' she announced.

Jardine looked up with more than a flicker of interest. 'I wonder what she wants?'

Jackie smiled brightly. 'We're never going to know unless we go and find out.' She picked up a notebook and headed for the door.

Jardine followed her out of the office, grateful for her enthusiasm.

Morag Nielson frowned slightly at the sight of Jackie Reid, finally conquering her instinctive aggression and dismissing it. She hadn't planned on having the young policewoman present, but it really didn't matter. She directed her attention to Jardine.

'There are a couple of things I didn't tell you about Douglas's murder. About Derek Amlot, actually,' she started.

Jardine pulled up a chair and sat opposite her, watching her face closely. 'What things, exactly?'

Morag drew a breath, checking over her story in her mind. 'The affair, between Derek and me. It's not the first time. There were others before me.'

'You mean with other wives?' Jardine asked, trying to sound more interested than he felt. It had been a disappointing start. He had been secretly hoping for some major revelation, or at least some important new evidence. Now it seemed that Morag Nielson only wanted to spill the beans on her boyfriend.

'And employees,' Morag went on. 'Young girls, some of them.'

Jardine's ears pricked up. This was definitely getting more interesting. 'So, Derek Amlot is a bit of a ladies' man, is he?'

Morag nodded. 'And there's something else. Derek had a personal grudge against Landsberg Chemicals — the company which wanted to poach Douglas. He would have done anything to stop them reaping the benefits of my husband's research.'

Jackie Reid couldn't stop herself from cutting in. Perhaps it was female intuition, but there was suddenly something very different about Morag Nielson's whole demeanour. 'Why are you telling us all this now, Mrs Nielson?'

Morag shrugged the question off. 'It's not important. Not to me, anyhow. But I thought it might have some relevance for you.'

Jardine sat forward in his chair. 'You're saying that Amlot had a personal feud with Landsberg? Why?'

'It was something Douglas told me about, ages ago,' Morag said. 'It happened about four years ago. Landsberg planted a research worker in the Casco laboratories — sort of industrial espionage in a way. Anyhow, they managed to steal a jump on a very important breakthrough which Derek was on the verge of investing heavily in. It cost him millions, apparently.'

Jardine digested Morag's little speech carefully. He glanced sideways at Jackie Reid. The look on her face confirmed the importance and the possible significance of this new information.

He returned his attention to Morag, staring her straight in the eye. 'Mrs Nielson. Derek Amlot says that he was at home with his wife and family on the night your husband was killed. His wife confirms his story. Now, do you have any evidence which would lead us to doubt this?'

It was a question Morag had been prepared for, just as she had prepared her response. She let out a contemptuous little laugh. 'He has that woman completely under his thumb. She'd say anything to protect him.' She shifted in her chair. She had planted the seeds of doubt, and now it was time to leave them to take root. She rose to her feet. 'Well, that's all I had to tell you. It's not much, but I thought it might be important.'

'Yes, thank you. You've been most helpful,' Jardine said, mouthing the standard spiel whilst concealing the true depth of his interest. He showed Morag to the door and escorted her out of the interview room.

When he returned Jackie Reid gave him a knowing grin. 'Hell hath no fury as a woman scorned,' she said.

Jardine looked thoughtful. 'Do you think that's all it was?' he asked uncertainly.

Jackie nodded emphatically. 'Amlot's dumped her — I'd bet my life on it,' she stated firmly. 'Now she's trying to get back at him by dishing the dirt.'

Jardine was far from convinced that that was all there was to it. 'But I can't see her making up stories like that,' he muttered. 'And even if there's only a grain of truth there, it throws a whole new light on things.'

Jackie gave him a slightly superior smile. 'Oh, I didn't say that it wasn't true,' she said quietly. 'In fact, I don't doubt her story for a second. What I am saying is we shouldn't, perhaps, take it at face value. Or, for that matter, make any basic assumptions about her motives.'

Jardine shook his head in confusion. 'I'm not sure I'm with you,' he admitted.

'There is such a thing as misdirection,' Jackie pointed out. 'We women can be devious creatures.'

Jardine regarded her with a strange mixture of exasperation and respect. 'You can say that again.'

Jill Cramer was another powerful lady who had long ago mastered the arts and wiles of her gender. Like a mother spider guarding her web, she sat in her usual corner of the Plaza East Hotel lobby, watching the front entrance and waiting for another fat and juicy fly to drop in.

A man pushed through the swing doors, took a few tentative steps into the lobby and paused, glancing around uncertainly as though searching for someone. Jill interpreted the signs. Rising from her armchair, she stepped forward to greet him, her hand outstretched.

'Mr Gregory? I'm Jill Cramer, of Management Quest. You're early.'

The man accepted her proffered handshake, then produced an ID card from his pocket and showed it to her. 'Wrong,' he said. 'Detective Chief Inspector Taggart, Maryhill Police Station.'

Jill Cramer was flustered, and it showed. 'Sorry, but I was expecting the chairman of the Alan King Corporation.'

'Then you'll have to make do with me until he gets here,' Taggart said. 'I called your offices. They told me where to find you.' He broke off, turning round slowly to review the luxurious surroundings. 'This is your private hunting ground, is it?'

Jill bristled slightly. 'This is where I meet a lot of my business clients, yes.'

'Is this where you met Dr Douglas Nielson of Casco Pharmaceuticals?'

Jill recognised the name. At the same time she understood the reason for Taggart's unscheduled visit. 'Yes, I read about his death. It was very tragic,' she said softly. She turned towards her little corner, indicating it with a wave of her hand. 'Perhaps you'd better come and sit down.'

Taggart followed her and sank into a chair. Jill was already summoning the ever-hovering waiter. 'Can I offer you a drink, Mr Taggart?'

Taggart shook his head. 'No thanks.' The waiter looked quite put out, turning away as though he had received a personal affront.

'So, it seems you're in a high-risk business,' Taggart said, struggling to sit upright in the unaccustomed luxury of the plush furniture. 'Do nasty things happen to many of your . . . clients — is that what you call them?'

Jill was guarded. 'I'm not sure what you mean.'

'You're in the business of poaching,' Taggart said, spelling it out for her. 'Stealing personnel on behalf of other companies. Doing their dirty work for them, basically.'

Jill Cramer glared at him. 'There's nothing dirty about wanting the best people for your company,' she said defensively.

'But some employees can be too valuable to lose. Especially, it seems, in the scientific field. Which happens to be the area you specialise in,' Taggart pointed out. He gave up the battle with the chair and sank back into it, relaxing. 'So how does your operation work, exactly?'

'Usually, the company they are currently working for offers to top the salary the new company is offering. Sweeteners are offered. There's a bit of financial bartering. Sometimes they take them, sometimes they don't.'

'And sometimes, as in the case of Dr Nielson, they don't get a chance,' Taggart put in.

Jill regarded him piercingly. 'Are you suggesting that Dr Nielson was killed to stop him leaving?'

'Does it happen?' Taggart countered.

Jill's first reaction was a vehement denial. The mere suggestion seemed ludicrous. And yet . . .

'There was a case a few years back,' she admitted after a thoughtful pause. 'A suspicious death, that's all. He was a computer services manager for the defence contractor, Gairlockhart. I met him on behalf of a Dutch firm. He was found drowned in the sea off Helensburgh, despite being an excellent swimmer.'

Taggart nodded. He vaguely remembered reading about the case. He glanced over to the front doors of the hotel where a smartly dressed man had just entered and was looking about himself uncertainly.

Taggart forced himself out of his chair. 'I think another rabbit just ran into the snare,' he muttered. 'Thanks for your help, Miss Cramer.'

He strode across the hotel lobby. Behind him, Jill Cramer rose to greet her new client, the fixed smile on her face and the standard welcoming speech forming on her lips. The waiter, alert as ever, changed direction in mid-stride and began to head towards her private corner.

Chapter Twenty-one

Carl Young looked exhausted, but triumphant. The second finished face stood proudly on the work-top, next to the bust of Janet Gilmour. It was a particularly striking face, Taggart thought, as he looked at it.

'You've done well,' he muttered, more than impressed.

Carl Young smiled proudly. 'I knew you were in a hurry for it, so I worked all through last night,' he said. He touched the face gently with his fingertips, pointing out several features. 'It's the best I can do to create a face which could be recognisable. As with the other one, I had to invent the ears, the shape of the lips and the hairstyle — but the actual structure of the face is quite distinctive. These very prominent cheekbones, for instance, and the shape of the eye sockets. The girl must have had a quite pronounced Asiatic look.'

Taggart summoned over the police photographer, who had been waiting for the official go-ahead. 'I want good full-face and profile shots, and perhaps a couple taken from a slight angle. After that, it's up to you, you're the expert.'

He turned back to Young. 'Thanks for your extra time. It's appreciated. I'll approve something extra added on to the agreed fee if you like.'

Young shook his head. 'That won't be necessary. I did it for Peter as much as anybody. As long as it's enough to provide him with a decent memorial, I'll be satisfied.'

Taggart looked at the face again, temporarily thrown into sharp relief by the flash of the photographer's camera. 'You learned well from him,' he complimented the man. He nodded at the bust of Janet Gilmour. 'Oh, by the way — Janet's mother asked if she could have the bust you did of her daughter?'

Young seemed slightly surprised. 'She likes it that much? I would have thought it was a bit morbid.'

Taggart tended to agree with him but said nothing.

'Well, of course, she'd be more than welcome to it,' Young went on. 'In fact, I'll make a cast for her — you might need the original for evidence in any future trial.'

Taggart looked at him gratefully. 'Thanks. I'm sure she'll be pleased with that.'

The photographer finished taking his last shot. 'That's about it, sir. I take it you want them developed right away.'

Taggart nodded. 'As fast as you like. And make sure that you get copies out to all the newspapers. With luck, we'll make the early afternoon edition.'

He took one last look at the second face. Someone, somewhere out there had to recognise the girl. Without that, they were still fighting demons in the dark.

Annie Gilmour looked out of her window as a car pulled up outside the house. She did not recognise the young man who got out carrying a cardboard box. He walked up the drive and rang the bell.

A slight frown creased Annie's forehead. She was not expecting any delivery. Puzzled, she went to answer the door.

'Mrs Gilmour? I brought this for you,' the stranger said. 'Can

I bring it in. It's quite heavy.' He suddenly seemed to notice the dubious expression on her face and smiled gently.

'Sorry, I didn't explain. I'm Carl Young. I did the reconstruction of your daughter's face. Mr Taggart said you would like it, so I made a copy for you.'

Annie's doubts lifted, to be replaced with a grateful smile. 'Oh, please — come in.' She led the way into Janet's bedroom, where she had already polished and prepared a place for the bust on the dressing table. 'Could you put it there, please?'

Young laid the box on the floor and lifted out the cast, mounted on a display pedestal. He set it down gently where Annie indicated and stepped back. 'As I said, it had to be a copy. The original might have to be used as an exhibit if there is a trial.'

Annie looked at him blankly, as though the concept had never occurred to her. 'Trial?' she repeated.

'Yes — of whoever killed her,' Young said.

Annie didn't seem to be listening. The dreamy, detached look which Taggart had noted previously had come over her face. 'This was her room,' she murmured. 'I've kept it just as it was. Kept it ready for her — for when she came back.'

Young regarded her with a slightly worried expression. The woman's odd reaction unnerved him slightly.

'I wonder if you know what you've done for me?' Annie went on. She paused to stare fondly at the bust for some time. 'You must have known her,' she said finally, in a strange tone.

Young started. It sounded almost like an accusation. 'It's a science, that's all,' he said, as though defending himself. 'I only carried on where Professor Hutton left off.'

'She was beautiful, wasn't she?' Annie asked, still in that strange tone. She opened one of the drawers in the dressing-table and drew out the golden sun amulet. Gently, she hung it around the neck of the bust. 'There. I think she'd want to wear the sun, now that she's home.' Annie turned to Carl Young again. 'She had two, you know. A sun and a moon. Which one she wore depended on the mood she was in. She was wearing the moon on the night she disappeared.'

Young glanced at the photograph of Janet on the dressing-table. In it she was wearing both charms on golden chains around her neck. He turned to Annie, smiling gently. 'Yes, Mrs Gilmour. She was very beautiful indeed.'

But Annie was off again, in the private world she had chosen to share with her dead daughter. It was a very small world, Young realised. There really wasn't any room for anyone else.

He picked up the empty cardboard box from the floor and backed away silently, leaving Annie staring lovingly at the bust. He let himself out of the house, not sorry to leave.

Chapter Twenty-two

Maureen MacDonald returned from a late lunch-break and pulled into her private parking space in the far corner of the Casco carpark. Retrieving her handbag and briefcase from the rear seat, she got out and walked across towards the main entrance to the administration building, pausing just inside the door as she remembered she had forgotten to lock the car.

She was about to return to the car when the receptionist looked across, recognised her and waved her over.

'Mr Amlot told me to ask you if you'd be good enough to go up to the venom extraction lab as soon as you got in,' the receptionist said. 'We have somebody working up there, and he wanted you to see that he doesn't cause any unnecessary damage.'

Maureen sucked at her teeth in a gesture of vexation. On top of everything else, now she was expected to be a works overseer. However, Derek Amlot did have a valid point. They were having to break in to the herpetarium, and it probably wasn't wise to have an unsupervised workman in a room full of venomous snakes.

She headed for the toxinology lab, the car forgotten. As she neared the lab, she could hear the sound of a heavy-duty drill. It would appear that the man had already started work.

The workman was drilling into the security lock on the herpetarium door, the noise of the drill drowning out the sound of Maureen's entrance. He jumped in sudden fright as he sensed her walk up behind him. He switched off the drill, laying it on the floor. 'Heavens, lady. You gave me a right turn there,' he complained.

'Sorry,' Maureen said. 'I didn't mean to disturb you.'

The man grinned good-naturedly, jerking his thumb in the direction of the snake tanks. 'I'm already disturbed, with all those creepy-crawlies in there. That hissing sound gives me the willies. That's why I started to get on with the job. The noise of the drill drowns 'em out.'

He gestured to the security lock. 'Seems an awful waste of money, breaking this open. It looks brand new to me — and they don't come cheap, these coded security jobs.'

Maureen agreed with him. It was a waste — but unfortunately necessary. The lock was brand new, having been fitted only a few days previously, after the break-in. The trouble was, only Dr Nielson and Christine Gray had known the new combination.

'Oh, well, we'll soon be in there,' the workman said, picking up his drill again. 'I just hope none of them reptiles is crawling about loose in there. I hate snakes.'

'Don't worry, they're all quite safe,' Maureen assured him. The drill started up again. The shrill squeal of metal against metal set her teeth on edge. She started to back away, her eyes falling on the workman's copy of the afternoon paper lying on top of his tool-box. Maureen bent down, picking it up, intending to take it to the comparative peace of one of the offices to read.

Taggart's luck had been in. The photograph of the second girl had, after all, made the early afternoon edition. A large reproduction of it took prominence on the front page.

Maureen stared at the photograph, a slightly nauseous feeling starting up deep in her stomach. The face was distinctive, striking.

Not the sort of face anyone would forget once they had seen it.

And Maureen *had* seen it. Here, in this very building. About two and a half years before.

She stared at the photograph again, almost praying that she had made a mistake. It was impossible. Maureen clearly remembered those slightly slanted eyes, the cheekbone structure which suggested some oriental cross-breeding somewhere in the bloodline. The girl's hair had been different, drawn up into a tight bun at the nape of the neck, but the face was unforgettable. Maureen even remembered her name, and her unusual accent.

It was all quite eerie. Feeling a little shaken, Maureen headed for Amlot's office.

'Are you sure you're not just imagining this?' Amlot said, gazing down at the newspaper Maureen had dumped on his desk.

'I'm not in the habit of imagining dead girls, Derek,' Maureen said, a little testily. She had recovered herself now, and Amlot's attitude was annoyingly patronising. 'Her name was Mary Hulme, and I interviewed her for a lab assistant's job about two and a half years ago. She was going to work with Dr Nielson and Christine Gray.'

'So why didn't she?' Amlot asked.

Maureen racked her brains for the exact details. There had been something a little odd about Mary Hulme, and she struggled to remember. It came at last. 'That's right — I remember now. She accepted the job, but she said she needed a few days to find a place to live. I distinctly remember her asking me if I knew anywhere close by where there were rooms to let. Anyway, she never turned up on the day she was due to start. In the end we decided that we could get along without another lab assistant and didn't advertise the post again.' Maureen paused, looking directly at Amlot. 'In fact, it was you who made that decision, as I recall. You thought that the project wasn't promising enough at that stage to justify another salary.'

Amlot looked away, returning his eyes to the newspaper. 'I don't remember,' he said. 'It would have been just one of a hundred day-to-day decisions.' He stared at the photograph again. 'This is only a reconstruction, you know. And anyone could be mistaken after this length of time.'

Maureen was adamant. 'Derek, I am not mistaken. I have a very good memory for faces. Her name was Mary Hulme, and she came from New Zealand. Christchurch, actually.'

'What do you plan to do?' Amlot asked. He seemed quite concerned.

'Tell the police, I suppose,' Maureen answered. 'I'll drop in this evening, after I've collected the kids from school.' She picked up the newspaper from Amlot's desk. 'Better take this back, I suppose. And check if that locksmith has opened the herpetarium yet. The snakes will need feeding.'

Taggart was driving past Annie Gilmour's florist's shop, on his way back to the station. There was a free parking space just ahead on the left-hand side of the road. On impulse, Taggart pulled into it and switched the engine off. Perhaps the news that Carl Young was making her a cast of Janet's face might cheer her up a little. She had seemed particularly strange the last time he had seen her.

He crossed the road to the shop. It was empty, with a 'CLOSED' sign hanging in the window. Taggart glanced at his watch. It was three-fifteen. Too late for a lunch-break and too early for Annie to have shut up shop for the day.

With a slightly worried frown, Taggart stepped into the news-agent's shop next door. 'Excuse me, do you know where Annie is?' he asked the young woman behind the counter.

She shook her head. 'The shop's been closed since yesterday. She didn't say anything to me about going away. She's had deliveries, too.'

Maureen MacDonald posted a security guard on the herpetarium and gathered her things together. She consulted the wall clock, noting that it was almost half-past three. The locksmith had taken longer than expected, and waiting around for him to finish had thrown her behind schedule. She would have to rush if she was to pick up the kids.

She hurried out of the building and across the carpark. Opening the car door, she threw her briefcase and handbag casually on to the front passenger seat, climbed in, slid the keys into the ignition and started the engine.

The motor purred into life, the momentary whirring of the starter and the initial firing of the engine drowning out another fainter sound. Although semi-torpid and sluggish with the cold, a Black Mamba managed to give a single hissing warning as it reacted to the sudden intrusion.

The warning went unnoticed. Maureen slipped the car into gear and drove off as the snake settled down again beneath her seat.

Taggart rang Annie Gilmour's doorbell for the third time, receiving no answer. He stepped back, looking up at the front of the house to where an upstairs bedroom window was half-open. He glanced down at the doorstep, noting the two bottles of milk which had not been taken in. Turning, he confirmed that Annie's van was parked in the street.

With a rising sense of foreboding, Taggart moved to the door again, bending down and peering through the flap of the letterbox. A few unopened letters and advertising leaflets lay on the welcome mat, unopened and unread.

The sense of foreboding hardened into a cold, certain knowledge that something was terribly wrong. Taggart stepped back, raised his foot and delivered a savage kick to the lock on the front door. The lock gave with a shriek of metal and a splintering of wood. The door flew open.

Cautiously, Taggart stepped into the house, every sense on edge and alert. 'Annie?' he called, not really expecting an answer. The house was deathly silent, except for the faint ticking of a wall-clock in the hallway.

Taggart moved to the foot of the stairs, resting his hand on the banister rail and placing one foot on the first step. He called again. 'Annie — it's me, Jim Taggart.'

His face set and grim, Taggart began to climb the stairs.

She was, as he had half-expected to find her, in Janet's bedroom. Annie lay sprawled on the bed, still and silent. Taggart's eyes swept the room in an instant, noting the bust of Janet proudly displayed on the dressing-table, the curtains in the half-open window swirling faintly in the breeze and the glass of water and empty medicine bottle. There was also an envelope propped up against a table-lamp with the single word 'Jim' scrawled upon it.

Taggart snatched up a small hand mirror from the dressing-table. Kneeling beside the bed, he held it to Annie's still lips, checking for any signs of breath. He grasped her wrist, feeling for the faintest, fluttering sign of a pulse. Finally, he lifted one of her closed eyelids gently and looked into her lifeless eye.

'Oh, Annie,' he sighed, hopelessly. He stood, slowly feeling the tears of bitterness and frustration swelling in his eyes. Blinking them away, he crossed to the dressing-table and picked up the letter, opening it and pulling out the single, folded sheet of paper inside.

The note was brief.

Dear Jim
You'll want to know why. The truth is, I've nothing left to want. Janet's come home to me and I'm happy that we're all reunited.
Thanks for being such a good friend over the years.
Annie

Taggart sank down on to the bed, beside Annie's body. Reaching out, he held her cold hand in his and squeezed it gently.

'Oh, Annie,' he muttered again, his voice choked.

There seemed no point in trying to hold back the tears which so desperately needed release. Taggart gave up fighting his emotions and indulged himself in the comfort of weeping for a dead friend.

The car engine had warmed up enough now to switch the heater on, Maureen MacDonald decided. The children would be cold from waiting around outside the school. They would appreciate a nice warm, cosy car to climb into. She tripped the switch on the dashboard. Assisted by the fan, waves of hot air began to heat up the interior of the car.

Beneath the seat, the Black Mamba stirred, reacting to the sudden change in temperature.

Maureen checked her watch as she pulled up outside the school gates. It was exactly three-fifty. She had managed to make it seconds before the children started to pour out of school. Knowing that her two daughters were almost always in the first wave of grateful escapees, Maureen left the car engine ticking over, the heater continuing to pulse out waves of heated air.

The Black Mamba, now fully awake and active, uncoiled itself beneath her seat and slithered into the rear of the car, seeking a more comfortable resting place. Its tongue flicking in and out furiously, it glided across the carpeted floor and up to the sculptured contours of the rear seat, attracted by the soft pile of the upholstery.

Maureen waved cheerily as her two daughters appeared, running across the school playground towards the gates. Her pleasure was marred only slightly by the fact that they appeared to have young Suzie McGregor in tow, no doubt on the promise of another lift home. Despite her daughter Marie's frequent insistence that it was 'on the way home', running Suzie back involved a two-and-a-half-mile detour. However, it was a minor inconveniece. Smiling, Maureen got out of the car to greet them.

She stooped over, hugging them. 'Have a good day?' she enquired, as she always did.

Fiona, her younger daughter, frowned. 'Apart from maths,' she complained. 'And Janie Ferguson wouldn't play with me at play-time.'

Marie clutched at her arm. 'Can we give Suzie a lift, Mummy? It's on the way home.'

Maureen smiled good-naturedly. 'Oh, I should think so.'

Whooping with pleasure, the three girls ran for the car. Fiona grabbed the rear door handle, wrenching the door open.

Maureen seized her by the arm, admonishing her. 'Now that's not how we behave when we have guests, is it? We have to be polite. Now, let Suzie in first.'

Fiona stepped back sheepishly, allowing her sister's friend to go in front of her.

Suzie began to clamber into the back of the car. Her eyes fell upon the large black snake curled up on the seat. For a second there was no reaction other than the vague thrill of shock and fear. It was a trick, a joke — a fake rubber snake which Marie had probably put there to frighten her.

Then the Black Mamba moved, rearing up into a threatening posture and Suzie began to scream hysterically.

The child's piercing cries were instantly taken up by Fiona, who had also seen the snake. With the uncanny speed of a mother reacting to danger threatening her young, Maureen saw and identified the threat and moved to thwart it. In a flash she had knocked Fiona aside and was reaching into the interior of the car to snatch the terrified Suzie to safety.

The Mamba struck with lightning speed even as Maureen's hands closed around the child's waist. Maureen pulled the child out of the car, kicking the door closed with her foot. Backing away, she set the hysterical child down on the pavement, screaming at the top of her voice. 'Get back, children! Get back!'

Only when the three children had recovered themselves sufficiently to retreat to a safe distance from the car did Maureen pay attention to herself. In horror she stared down at the blood oozing from the twin puncture marks on the back of her hand.

'Oh, my God,' she sobbed weakly, feeling her legs begin to buckle under her. The noise of the children screaming and crying was like the sounds of a distant battle inside her head. Her senses were swimming. Shock and pain overcame her. As everything turned black, Maureen MacDonald collapsed to the pavement in a faint.

Inside the car, the Black Mamba slithered up the back of the seat and across the hatch cover, coiling itself defensively against the glass of the rear window.

Jackie Reid answered the telephone, her face registering shock as she received the terse message from ambulance control.

She dropped the phone, shouting across at Jardine, who was busy with paperwork. 'We've got another snake attack.'

Jardine looked up, instantly alert. 'Who is it this time?'

'It's Casco's research director, Maureen MacDonald. They're rushing her to the intensive care unit right now,' Jackie told him.

Jardine was on his feet in a flash, his mind racing to get the correct sequence of moves in place. 'Get hold of Sullivan,' he snapped. 'We need to identify the snake. I'll meet you there. Then contact Taggart and tell him what's happened.'

Jardine began to head for the door as Jackie reached for the phone again to carry out his instructions. He paused, with a sudden thought. 'And tell Taggart that it has to be Amlot,' he said with cold certainty in his voice. 'Amlot's the key to this whole business, I'm sure of it.'

Chapter Twenty-three

As ever, Derek Amlot seemed to accept the news about Maureen MacDonald stoically, almost without emotion. Apart from a muttered expression of concern and a half-hearted enquiry into her condition, he appeared to regard the whole business as merely another burdensome pressure upon him — something which was unfortunate, but beyond his control.

Taggart eyed him piercingly, searching for anything which would give him a clue to understanding the man. Amlot's eyes betrayed nothing, his normal, fixed expression of vague harassment preventing enlightenment.

Taggart found him infuriating. Yet, despite Jardine's obvious conviction that he was the killer, he remained unconvinced. If anything, Amlot was *too* cold-blooded to be a murderer, he thought. In Taggart's experience, killers needed some degree of passion, at least a hint that their self-control could snap. Amlot showed no sign of either.

For the moment Taggart sat back, letting McVitie control the interrogation. His superior had insisted on coming along, and Taggart had not objected. Perhaps a fresh mind might prise something significant out of the man, although Taggart somehow doubted it.

'Tell us again — what exactly did Maureen MacDonald say to you?' McVitie was saying.

Amlot sighed wearily. 'I've told you. She said that the girl's name was Mary Hulme. She had apparently applied for a job here about two and a half years ago and Maureen had interviewed her. She was offered the position, but she didn't show up on her first day.'

'Which department was she going to work in?' McVitie asked.

'In toxinology. With Dr Nielson.'

Taggart stirred from his quiescent state. 'And you told her that she might be wasting our time?' he demanded angrily.

Again, Amlot showed no real response. 'I told her she could be mistaken,' he corrected.

'This girl must have had a personnel file opened on her,' McVitie put in. 'Perhaps that might tell us more about her.'

Amlot shook his head. 'Maureen checked that, I believe. It was missing, probably thrown away. Our records department would only have reason to keep it if she had stayed with us.'

Taggart could not quite believe that the whole business could be dismissed so casually. 'Weren't there any checks made on her? As to why she didn't show up, what might have happened to her?'

'I can't tell you that for sure, but I very much doubt it,' Amlot said calmly. 'People come for an interview, you think that they're interested — then they go somewhere else and get a better offer. It's not uncommon.'

There was one question which McVitie hadn't asked. Taggart put it now. 'Did you ever meet this Mary Hulme yourself? Either in the course of work or socially?' Taggart looked Amlot straight in the eyes, waiting for an answer.

Amlot returned his stare with a cool, level gaze. 'No, I never saw the girl. If I had done, I would have remembered, wouldn't I?'

Taggart looked away from the man, appealing to McVitie. There didn't seem much point in carrying the interrogation any further.

'We're getting nowhere, sir,' he muttered.

McVitie stood up. 'I agree with you.' He looked down at Amlot. 'No doubt Detective Chief Inspector Taggart will want to talk to you again.'

Amlot shrugged carelessly. 'I can't see why,' he said. 'There's really nothing more I can tell you.'

Taggart wasn't so sure. 'I'll be the judge of that,' he said. It was not quite a warning, not quite an accusation.

DC Reid stared into the back of Maureen MacDonald's car, fascinated by the cold, black eyes of the snake regarding her malevolently through the rear window. 'Well, it doesn't look like an Eastern Diamond rattlesnake, the Saw-Scaled viper has already turned up — so it must be the other Black Mamba,' she observed.

Jardine was looking away. He had seen enough snakes to last him a lifetime. 'You'll be getting a degree in natural history after this,' he said. He turned to Sullivan. 'Well?'

Sullivan stared through the glass at the snake. 'That's a Black Mamba all right,' he confirmed. 'Vicious biters. Those fangs can sink into muscle tissue like it was butter.'

Jardine didn't want to hear the details. 'You're absolutely sure? We need the correct anti-venom.'

Almost reluctantly, Sullivan tore his eyes away from the snake. 'No doubt about it. That's a Mamba all right.' He brandished his rubber-tipped tongs. 'Want me to bag it for you?'

Jardine nodded. He turned to Jackie. 'After Sullivan's finished, switch off the car engine and stay here until the fingerprint people get here. Not that they're going to find anything, but we have to follow procedure.'

'Always wears gloves, does he?' Sullivan muttered, overhearing the conversation.

'Yes, he's careful, this one,' Jackie Reid said.

Sullivan winked at her. 'Or maybe he's just frightened of snakes?' he suggested.

Jardine flashed him a slightly surprised look. It was a possibility that none of them had considered.

Taggart rushed into McVitie's office without knocking, waving a sheet of fax paper in his hand.

'Sir, the Met had a missing person file on Mary Hulme. She came to this country from New Zealand just over three years ago with a PhD in molecular genetics. She worked for about six months for a company in London and then quit. After that, she just disappeared. Her parents filed the missing person report a year later.'

'Anything to connect her with Glasgow?' McVitie asked.

Taggart shook his head. 'Nothing on her file. She had no friends, no relatives — in fact no reason at all to come up here.'

'Unless she saw a job advertised by Casco, and came up on the spur of the moment,' McVitie suggested.

'Aye,' Taggart nodded. 'She took all her clothes and possessions from the bedsit she had in North London, so she must have been planning to find somewhere to stay up here.'

Taggart was silent for a while as a sudden thought struck him. He sat down opposite McVitie, facing him squarely with an excited expression on his face.

'Don't you see, sir? That's the connection. Janet Gilmour walked out of her home after a row with her parents. She didn't stay with friends, or any of the people you'd expect her to go to. So maybe she looked for a flat, or a bedsitter somewhere? Somewhere that was advertised. Somewhere that Mary Hulme also found, a year and a half later.'

McVitie considered the suggestion deeply for several moments, finally nodding thoughtfully. 'You could be right, Jim.'

Taggart slammed his fist down on the desk. 'Damn it, sir. I *know* I'm right. It's the only answer that makes sense. All this time we've been assuming that there was some direct connection between the two victims. There never was one — except that both girls met the same killer.'

'Well, now that we have two names, perhaps we can start to get somewhere,' McVitie muttered. 'I guess we're just lucky that Carl Young was able to create such accurate likenesses of the two victims.'

He broke off, regarding Taggart sadly. 'I know that this case has meant a lot to you personally, Jim.'

Taggart's face fell. 'You mean Annie Gilmour?'

'Yes, and I'm sorry,' McVitie said gently.

Taggart sighed. 'Ah well, maybe it doesn't do to get too close to the dead, sir.'

McVitie shot him a strange, almost reprimanding look. 'Or too close to the bereaved, Jim.'

Chapter Twenty-four

Colin Murphy was going through his routine with the python yet again, to the delight of a bunch of happy, excited schoolchildren. Finally, he uncoiled the snake from around his neck and cradled it in his arms, passing it around the ring of children so that they could have a final stroke.

He glanced at his watch as he passed the snake around. It was past five-thirty. Time to close up for the day. He smiled apologetically at the children. 'Sorry, kids. That's it for today,' he announced.

Several of the children groaned with disappointment. Murphy looked miserable with them. He genuinely enjoyed their company, their uninhibited enthusiasm. 'Tell you what — I'll have another snake to show you tomorrow. An Indian rock python. How would you like that?' he suggested.

The promise seemed to brighten the children up again. Murphy smiled, pleased to have made them happy. He began to shoo the children out of the animal encounters enclosure.

Satisfied that the area was clear, he carried the python into the reptile house and returned it to its tank. He set the thermostat on the heating controls and went to check the breeding room, surprised to find Sullivan inside. He was admiring his newly caught Black Mamba.

'Good job I checked,' Murphy said. 'I was about to lock up. You ready to go yet?'

Sullivan shook his head, without bothering to look round. 'You go ahead. I have a few things to do. I've got my own set of pass keys.'

Murphy left him to it and returned to the main display area. The attractive young art student he had noticed several times over the last few days was still busily sketching a tank of salamanders. Murphy strolled up to her. 'Sorry, but it's chucking-out time.'

The girl looked up from her work, smiling as she recognised him. She had watched him entertaining the children for days now, and had been secretly hoping that he would notice her. Apart from his good looks, there was something about his gentle manner which she found particularly appealing.

'It's all right. I'd more or less finished.' She took the drawing off the easel and held it up for his inspection. 'Here, what do you think? Have I done them justice?'

Murphy looked at the sketch. 'They're very good. I like the way you've managed to capture the texture of their skin.'

The girl preened slightly under praise. 'They're so beautiful. I find them fascinating.'

'You should see the Phyllobates,' Murphy told her. 'They're even prettier.'

The word meant nothing to the girl. 'What are they?'

'Dendrobatids . . . Poison Arrow frogs. There are a lot of different species.'

The girl frowned slightly. 'I must have missed them.'

Murphy nodded towards the breeding area. 'We don't have any out here in the main display area. We keep them in there, but unfortunately there's someone working in there with venomous snakes, so I can't let you in.'

The girl looked disappointed.

'Actually, I keep some at home,' Murphy said. 'They're a sort of hobby of mine.'

The girl's eyes widened slightly. 'Aren't they dangerous?'

'Not if you handle them right. It's their skin secretions which can kill you. The South American Indians rub their poison on their darts.'

'I've been watching you handle that python,' the girl confessed. 'You do it very well. The kids love it.'

Murphy grinned. 'They get all excited. They think he's dangerous, but really he's just a big softy.'

Despite his modesty the girl was still impressed. 'Well, I think you're very good.'

Murphy shrugged, looking a little embarrassed. 'It's a knack. I seem to get on well with kids.'

The girl looked up at him, now openly flirting. 'I bet you get on well with just about everybody. Especially girls.' She held out her hand. 'My name's Madeleine. My friends mostly call me Maddy. I suppose I am, a bit.'

Murphy took her hand shyly. 'I'm Colin,' he said simply, giving it a nervous little shake.

Madeleine held his hand for longer than was strictly necessary, giving him the full treatment with her big blue eyes at the same time. 'I'd love to see these . . . what did you call them?'

'Phyllobates,' Murphy reminded her. He shifted his feet awkwardly, more than a little overpowered by her openly flirtatious manner. She was obviously giving him a come-on, but he wasn't sure how to respond. Kids were much easier to deal with. You simply came down to their open, innocent level.

'I suppose you could come home with me, and I'll show you mine,' he suggested nervously.

Madeleine giggled, clutching at his arm. 'You show me yours and I show you mine — right?' she joked suggestively.

Murphy flushed. 'I . . . didn't mean . . . ' he stammered, embarrassed.

Madeleine saw his discomfiture and was annoyed with herself.

He was obviously painfully shy and she had upset him. She squeezed his arm gently, reassuringly.

'It's all right, Colin. I was only joking,' she said gently. 'I'd love to come back and see these . . . Phyllobates of yours.'

Releasing him, she began to pack up her easel and drawing materials. Tucking them away into a satchel, she slung it over one shoulder and took his arm again.

Still a little uncertain, Murphy let her guide him towards the zoo exit.

Jardine looked in through the window to the intensive care unit, where a nurse was bending over Maureen MacDonald injecting the serum into her arm. He turned away to face Taggart, who had been pacing up and down the corridor anxiously. 'They're giving her the anti-venom now, sir. Let's hope we can save her.'

Taggart's face was grim. 'We have to save her. She's the only one now who can give us the answers we need.'

Jardine nodded thoughtfully. 'Like why three people had to die to prevent two faces being identified.'

'Oh no, Michael.' Taggart shook his head. 'Only one face. Mary Hulme's.' Aware that Jardine was regarding him curiously, he explained further. 'You see, there really never was any connection between Janet Gilmour and Mary Hulme. Only that they were both unfortunate enough to bump into the same murderer.'

Taggart began to walk along the hospital corridor. Jardine fell into step beside him. There was still one thing he didn't fully understand. 'But if this Mary Hulme died before she ever started working at Casco — then what was the point of killing Dr Nielson and Christine?' he asked.

'Good question,' Taggart muttered. 'Sorry I can't give you the answer. That's what puzzles me, too.'

'And the method used,' Jardine added. 'A bit hit and miss — or it could have been. Supposing either or both his victims had recovered? He'd have achieved nothing.'

Taggart suddenly stopped dead in his tracks. He glanced back, briefly, towards the intensive care unit, a thoughtful frown on his face. He took a few seconds to analyse the sudden thought which had popped into his head. Gelling it together into a theory which finally made sense, he turned back to face Jardine excitedly. 'Mike — I want you to take me to see these anti-venoms. Right now.'

Finding a new burst of energy, Taggart began to stride down the corridor towards the exit as though he were in a race.

Jardine was caught on the hop, left standing with a puzzled expression on his face. Halfway down the corridor Taggart stopped, turned around and yelled at him. 'Well, come on, then. We don't have any time to lose. We have to get to the Casco laboratory.'

Still slightly bemused, Jardine broke into a loping run to catch Taggart up as he started to move again. He was obviously on to something, Jardine thought — but what?

Wisely he didn't ask. He knew Taggart too well, and he recognised the look that the chief had on his face. He'd explain everything in his own good time.

Colin Murphy opened the door to his living-room and ushered Madeleine in. She crossed to the settee and dumped her satchel on it. Taking off her coat without waiting for an invitation, she draped it over one of the arms. She took a good look around the room.

'Well, this is nice,' she said politely. In fact, she found the room drab and depressing. A typical bachelor pad, she thought, having seen many. Her eyes fell upon the vivarium tank which seemed to take pride of place, on its own display stand in one corner of the room, and illuminated by a couple of tracking spotlights. 'Are they in that?' she asked, beginning to move towards it.

'Be careful,' Colin warned her. 'Don't try to take the cover off the top of the tank.'

Madeleine looked back at him, grinning. 'Don't worry. I'm not likely to try, after all the things you've told me.'

She reached the vivarium and peered through the glass. Inside the heated tank, some half a dozen brightly coloured little frogs were hopping about animatedly. Watching them, Madeleine could understand their appeal.

'They're gorgeous,' she said. 'Where on earth did you get them?'

Murphy crossed the room, standing behind her. 'From a licensed dealer,' he explained. 'Not everyone would be allowed to buy them, but I'm a member of the Dendrobatids Society.'

'Really,' Madeleine said, conversationally, not really interested. It all sounded terribly dull. In fact, she had begun to wonder if she had made a wise move in picking Colin up. For all his good looks and charm, he was not turning out to be the sort of man who knew how to give a girl a good time. He seemed far too shy, too studious, for her liking.

'Look, now that you're here – why don't I cook you a nice spaghetti bolognese?' Colin suggested. 'I do a very good one.'

Madeleine turned from the vivarium, slightly surprised to find him standing so close to her. Perhaps he was trying to raise the courage to make a pass at her, she thought.

She decided to help along a little. 'That sounds super,' she said, with faked enthusiasm. She raised herself slightly on her toes, pressed her face forward and kissed him full on the lips.

Murphy was unresponsive. In fact, Madeleine thought, he seemed almost afraid of her. She suddenly felt very foolish. She covered her own embarrassment with a bit of bluster. 'My, my – we really are the shy one, aren't we?' she said, her eyes slightly mocking.

Murphy turned his face away, looking down at the floor. 'Look, perhaps it would be better if you went,' he murmured awkwardly.

Madeleine considered the suggestion for several seconds. All her instincts told her he was right. There was obviously going to be no evening of passion, and she was not in the mood to seduce a shy and rather boring young man who only seemed to get excited about frogs.

However, there was another consideration. He had offered her a meal. She hadn't eaten since the previous evening, and times were hard when you were struggling to get by on a student grant. Selling her body in exchange for a plate of food was nothing new to her

— in fact she thoroughly enjoyed both pleasures. This seemed no different, except that she would probably have to forego sex afterwards. She decided to stay for the meal.

'Well, that's a fine thing,' she teased him. 'You invite a girl to stay for dinner and then you tell her to go. Not a very gentlemanly thing to do, I must say.'

Murphy was embarrassed even more. He shuffled his feet awkwardly. 'I'm sorry,' he muttered. 'Look — why don't you go upstairs and freshen up and I'll get the dinner on.'

Madeleine smiled with relief. For a moment there she had thought the evening was going to be a total washout. 'That's more like it,' she said sweetly, giving him an encouraging smile. She crossed the room and picked her satchel up from the settee, rummaging through it until she found her make-up bag.

'Which way?'

Murphy gestured to the door. 'Go up the stairs and turn left,' he said. 'You can't miss the bathroom. There's clean towels and everything.'

Madeleine headed for the door as Murphy walked into the kitchen and took a packet of minced beef out of the fridge.

Jardine opened the fridge door. Taggart peered over his shoulder as he pointed out the phials of anti-venom, all stacked in neat little rows and clearly marked with their respective identifying numbers.

'You see, sir, they're all here, and all marked.' Jardine drew Taggart's attention to the typed list stuck to the inside of the door. 'As you can see, some of these anti-venoms are what they call polyspecific.'

'What's that when the cat's finished with it?' Taggart interrupted.

'It means that one anti-venom can be used to cure the bite from several different types of snake,' Jardine explained. 'Others are more specialised — only effective against the venom of a particular species.'

Taggart digested this information carefully. He pushed the

fridge door shut, standing upright. He stared at his companion thoughtfully. 'Yet Professor Hutton wasn't cured — and neither was Christine Gray,' he pointed out.

Jardine nodded sadly. 'No, sir.' He waited patiently for Taggart to expound his theory.

It was not long in coming. Taggart tapped the fridge door with the back of his fingernails. 'Now, if our murderer knew enough about these creatures to only pick out the ones which were the most deadly — would it not be reasonable to assume that he also knew something about these anti-venoms as well. Do you agree, Michael?'

Jardine thought for a second, finally nodding in agreement. 'That makes sense.'

'Aye, I thought it would,' Taggart muttered. 'So — if he wanted to be absolutely sure that his victims would die, he'd stack the cards in his favour, wouldn't he?'

Jardine suddenly understood what Taggart was getting at. 'Of course,' he blurted out. 'He tampered with the anti-venoms. He wouldn't even have had to break the seals. All he had to do was to change the numbers around.' Jardine was silent for a while as the truth sank in. 'So, Christine got the antidote for the wrong type of venom. That's what killed her.'

He stared at Taggart, deeply shaken. In the long silence which followed there was an angry hissing sound in the background, like steam escaping from a pressure valve. 'What's that?' Taggart said, his eyes narrowing.

Jardine placed a finger over his lips. 'There's someone in the snake room,' he whispered. He began to creep slowly towards the herpetarium, with Taggart close on his heels.

The door was pulled shut, but the gaping hole in the wall next to it showed that the lock was still missing. Gently, Jardine pushed the door with his finger. It swung open without a sound. He edged into the room, in darkness except for the faint glow of lighting and heating elements in some of the snake tanks.

Taggart was not at all happy. He regarded the tanks and their contents with great distaste. His eyes sweeping the floor cautiously, he followed Jardine through a double row of glass tanks towards the back of the herpetarium.

There was another sound. A rustling, like somebody handling paper. Jardine froze, listening intently to pinpoint the source. Silently he turned to Taggart, jabbing his finger towards the rear wall of the room. He continued creeping along the row of tanks, pausing at the very end.

Satisfied that Taggart was covering him from behind, Jardine poised himself on the balls of his feet and sprang forward to confront the intruder.

With a sense of relief, he encountered only Dennis the tea-boy, who was sitting on a lab stool reading a comic by the light of one of the viper tanks.

The lad looked up in sudden alarm, his normally smiling face worried and shaken. Besides his obvious fright, he also looked guilty, Jardine thought. 'What are you doing in here, Dennis?' he asked sternly.

The lad seemed confused. 'I'm not doing anything wrong, honest. He told me to come in here, but I don't want to get him into trouble. He's a nice man.'

Taggart moved forward. 'Who told you, Dennis?' he asked softly.

'Mr Franks, the security man,' Dennis said, somewhat reluctantly. 'He asked me to stay here till the man putting the new lock on got back. He was supposed to stay but he was hungry. He went out to get something to eat.' He looked over at Jardine, a childish smile on his simple face. 'I should get a sheriff's badge, eh?'

Jardine relaxed. Dennis looked harmless enough, and his guilty look was probably not for himself but for the missing security guard.

'I used to come in here a lot,' Dennis went on. 'Dr Nielson used to let me come in and look at the snakes. I like snakes.'

'I know, Dennis. You told me earlier,' Jardine said gently.

Taggart flashed Jardine a vaguely critical glance. That was one little piece of information which his assistant hadn't seen fit to pass on. He turned to Dennis again. 'I expect there are lots of things you could tell us, Dennis, if you wanted to,' he suggested.

Dennis looked unsure. 'What sort of things?'

'Oh, all sorts of things,' Taggart muttered vaguely. 'I mean, you've been here a long time, you must know a lot of things that happen. People who have worked here, for instance.'

Dennis nodded.

'Do you ever remember Dr Nielson meeting a girl from New Zealand called Mary Hulme?' Taggart went on. 'She was going to come and work here for him as a research assistant.'

Dennis thought for a long time, his face strained with the effort of remembering. Finally, it brightened. 'New Zealand — yes, I do remember her,' he said. 'She talked funny. She was here for a couple of days.'

Taggart and Jardine exchanged a perplexed look. 'Are you sure of that, Dennis?' Jardine asked.

'Oh, yes.' Dennis seemed quite positive now. 'I remember her because she was nice and friendly.'

'Now, let's get this perfectly straight,' Taggart said. 'Are you telling us that Mary Hulme actually *worked* in this laboratory for a couple of days?'

Dennis nodded. 'I do remember, really. People think I'm stupid and can't remember things — but I can.'

'We don't think you're stupid, Dennis,' Taggart told him. 'Now — do you remember what happened to Mary?'

The young man's face fell. 'She never turned up. For her first day. She was nice, too.'

Taggart looked across at Jardine, an exasperated expression on his face. 'We don't seem to be getting anywhere here,' he muttered.

Jardine took it up. 'Dennis, listen to me,' he said in a gentle, friendly tone. 'If she never turned up on her first day — then how can she have worked here?'

Dennis seemed confused for a moment, then his face brightened. 'Oh, she wasn't really working here. She just came in for a couple of days to get to know the job. Before the Monday she was supposed to start. She was very keen.'

Unable to contain his excitement, Taggart leaned forward,

hardly daring to hope that Dennis would be able to answer his next question. 'Listen, Dennis — this is very, very important. Do you know where she lived?'

Dennis nodded his head. 'That's easy,' he said smiling. 'She was staying in Colin's house. He used to be a lab technician here.' He looked up at Jardine. 'That's what I would have liked to be, but I don't have the brains.'

Jardine gave him a smile of reassurance. 'Don't worry, Dennis — you're doing just fine. How did Colin explain her disappearance?'

'He said she'd changed her mind. Gone back to New Zealand.'

Taggart reached forward and patted Dennis on the shoulder. 'Son, you just won your sheriff's badge.'

He glanced at Jardine, who looked shell-shocked, hardly able to believe what he had just heard. 'Well?' he asked. 'Shall we go and catch ourselves a killer?'

Chapter Twenty-five

Sullivan was just locking the gates of the zoo as the car screamed to a halt outside the entrance and Taggart and Jardine jumped out.

He looked surprised to see them. 'What now? A couple of alligators loose in the Glasgow sewer system?'

There was no time for banter. 'Who else would keep an anti-venom for the Black Mamba?' Taggart snapped.

Sullivan thought for a second. 'I imagine there's one at Edinburgh Zoo. I shouldn't think there's one any nearer.'

'Get on to them. Tell them we need it here, now. We'll arrange for a car.'

'What happened?' Sullivan wanted to know.

'No time,' Jardine said hurriedly. 'Where's Murphy?'

Sullivan shrugged his shoulders. 'Long gone. He had company.'

'Company?' Jardine was on the alert instantly.

'Young blonde girl. Art student, I think. She's been hanging around here for a couple of days now.'

Jardine turned to his superior with a horrified expression on his face, but Taggart was already running back towards the car. He slid into the passenger seat and wound the window down as he waited for Jardine to rejoin him. 'Just get that anti-venom up here as fast as you can,' he called to Sullivan as Jardine jumped in beside him and pulled away from the kerb with a gut-churning squeal of rubber.

Sullivan stared after the departing car in total bewilderment for a while, then headed for his van to make a call on his mobile phone.

'I wonder how many others there were?' Jardine mused as he raced towards Murphy's house. 'How many other bodies we haven't found?'

Taggart shook his head in a hopeless, helpless gesture. 'Murphy had to kill his ex-colleagues from Casco simply because they could recognise Mary Hulme and connect him with her. He'd have done it, too — but he overlooked just one person. Or maybe he figured Dennis was too simple-minded to matter.'

'And Janet Gilmour? Where did she fit in?' Jardine asked.

Taggart shrugged his shoulders. 'After she walked out on her parents, she needed somewhere to stay. Who knows what led her to him? Perhaps just a chance meeting, with Murphy playing the sympathetic stranger.'

Jardine let out a short, bitter laugh at the irony of it all. 'Some sympathy. Nielson was the nearest thing he had to a friend, and he murdered him without a qualm.'

He trod down even harder on the accelerator and fell silent, concentrating on his driving and thinking of Christine Gray.

Murphy slid the diced onion and chopped green peppers into the frying pan, where the minced beef was already sizzling gently. He stirred in tomato purée, tasting the results by licking the end of his spatula. Not quite satisfied, he sprinkled in a little more oregano and tried again. It tasted better. Not his best, perhaps, but it would do.

He checked the pasta, bubbling away in a saucepan. It was still a little hard, slightly short of the *al dente* consistency for really good spaghetti.

Putting down his cooking utensils, he walked from the kitchen into the lounge, crossing to the door and shouting up the stairs. 'The dinner will be ready in about ten minutes.'

Madeleine's voice drifted down from the bathroom. 'It smells good. I'll be down in five.'

Murphy closed the door. He walked across to the sideboard and slid open one of the drawers, gazing lovingly at his precious little collection of souvenirs inside. His love tokens.

He reached in and picked out his favourite. Swinging it gently on the end of its gold chain, he marvelled again at the way the little crescent-moon amulet glinted as it caught the light.

Reluctantly, he replaced the necklace in the drawer, along with other pieces of jewellery and items of female underwear. Tucked neatly next to them lay a small pile of thin, disposable plastic gloves. Murphy picked up a pair and slipped them on, taking great care to check that he had not punctured either of them with his fingernails.

He crossed to the vivarium, lifting off the lid of the tank and placing it on the floor. Slowly, gently, he lowered his hand into the tank and scooped up one of the tiny, brightly coloured frogs in his palm.

With delicate precision, Murphy stroked one finger across the creature's glistening back, gently rubbing its skin with a slow, circular massaging motion. A few seconds was enough. Looking down at his gloved finger, Murphy noted the faint smears of a milky-white secretion with a smile of satisfaction. He replaced the frog in the vivarium and walked to the table, picking up a tablespoon. Holding it carefully in his other hand, he smeared the secretion around the inside of the bowl of the spoon and then laid it back on the table. He returned to the vivarium, replaced the lid and peeled off the plastic gloves very carefully. Holding them between his finger and thumb, he carried them into the kitchen, dropped them into the waste-bin and crossed to the sink to wash his hands thoroughly, finally drying them on a tear-off sheet of disposable kitchen towel.

Satisfied that he had taken all possible precautions, he returned to the cooking spaghetti and tested it again.

The meal was ready. Murphy took two large plates from the kitchen cupboard and served up two generous portions. He carried them into the lounge and laid them down on the dining table, just as Madeleine entered the room, looking vibrant and freshly made-up.

'Hey, that really does smell good,' she murmured appreciatively.

Murphy pulled out a chair for her. 'I'm good at spaghetti bolognese. I told you.' He took his own place at the table opposite her as she sat down. 'Well — tuck in. I think you'll like it.'

Madeleine didn't need much encouragement. She hadn't realised quite how hungry she actually was until the smell of the cooking had drifted up the stairs. Winding spaghetti round her fork, she lifted it to her mouth and began to eat voraciously.

Murphy held his own spoon and fork poised in the air, watching her. 'I don't think you're doing that quite right,' he said, his voice faintly accusatory.

Madeleine raised her eyes. 'What do you mean.'

Murphy nodded at the fork in her hand. 'Eating spaghetti just with a fork like that. I always use a spoon as well. It's the proper Italian way — and you don't get sauce dribbling down your chin.'

As if to demonstrate, he wound pasta around his own fork, transferred it to the bowl of his spoon and lifted both implements to his mouth together.

Madeleine frowned. She wasn't used to having her dinner companions criticise her table manners. Apart from which, she was becoming increasingly convinced that there was something very odd about Colin Murphy. But — if it made him happy . . .

With a faint shrug, she picked up her spoon and copied him. She was hungry enough to have eaten the meal with her fingers had he suggested it. 'This is a big house,' she murmured conversationally as she ate. 'Do you live here all on your own?'

Murphy nodded. 'It belonged to my parents. They both died about five years ago. I used to take in lodgers, but I stopped. You don't get any privacy.'

He fell silent, tucking into his food. Madeleine spooned in a few more mouthfuls and tried again.

'So — what made you get interested in frogs?'

Murphy looked up at her, his eyes suddenly bright and animated. 'It was the toxins that fascinated me. I used to work in a lab where we studied them. Snakes, spiders . . .'

Madeleine shuddered. 'Ugh, don't mention spiders to me. I hate them.'

But Murphy didn't seem to be listening. Obsessively, he carried on talking. 'My frogs, *Phylobates terribilis* – that's their full Latin name – have a really unique poison. Would you like to hear about it?'

Madeleine sighed, resigning herself. 'I've a feeling that I'm going to anyway,' she murmured.

'It's called a batrachotoxin,' Murphy continued. 'It's a neuromuscular poison which causes interference with the maintenance of cell membrane electrical polarisation. In short, muscular paralysis.'

'Charming,' Madeleine muttered sarcastically, applying herself to the spaghetti bolognese with renewed vigour, before he managed to put her off her food completely.

'The South American Indians roast them to extract the poison, but you can do it just by massaging their glands,' Murphy droned on.

Madeleine felt an involuntary shudder ripple through her body, which was vaguely unnerving. The room was warm, even too warm, so it had not been a normal shiver. Almost simultaneously, she was aware that her heart was pumping erratically.

Murphy continued his grisly narrative with almost sadistic glee. 'There's no antidote, and no treatment either. It's without doubt the most potent animal toxin known.' He paused, a dreamy look coming over his face. 'I think that's what fascinates me the most – that something so beautiful can be so deadly.'

Madeleine laid down her fork and spoon, staring at him with sudden alarm. Now her hearing seemed wrong, somehow distorted. Murphy's voice was different, strange. It had suddenly taken on an oddly detached, echoing, somewhat hypnotic tone — almost as if there was somebody else inside him, using his mouth as a loudspeaker.

Her earlier misgivings about Colin Murphy were now rapidly turning to open fear. He was no longer just odd, he was definitely menacing. 'I think I should be scared of you,' Madeleine said in a tiny, somewhat strangled voice.

Murphy stared at her with expressionless eyes. 'I'm like the python,' he said, smiling. 'Just a big softy.'

Madeleine pushed her plate away impulsively, her appetite completely gone. She tried to push her chair back and get to her feet, but her muscles didn't seem to be responding properly. The inside of her mouth felt strangely numb, like when you had an injection at the dentist.

'It's quite painless, really,' Murphy was saying. 'Your body just stops working and then you die.'

Terror-stricken and panicking now, Madeleine made another effort to get to her feet. For a second there was nothing then, suddenly, it was as if every nerve and muscle in her entire body was galvanised into action at once. With a massive convulsive shudder, her body jerked out of the chair and she collapsed on to the floor.

Murphy rose from his own chair slowly, coming round the table to stand over her. There was a bizarre, incongruous look on his face — part concern, part pity and part excitement. It was so close now — that sweet, delicious moment of death. Murphy's blood pulsed. He was acutely aware of the tightness in the crotch of his trousers, as his erection grew in anticipation.

'You mustn't try to fight it,' he said in a low, almost gentle voice. 'You'll just stop breathing. Please don't fight.'

Madeleine's body gave a series of violent spasms which jerked her across the carpet, until she lay half-propped up against the settee. Totally incapable of any controllable or voluntary movement, she could only stare up at Murphy through wide-open, totally terrified eyes.

The end came quickly. There was a moment of absolute and final horror, for although Madeleine could see perfectly, and her brain was functioning apparently normally, she suddenly realised that she was no longer breathing. There was no panic, no frantic struggle for breath, because the muscles of her chest and stomach were already inert and beyond control. In the last few seconds there was only the cold and terrible certainty of death, right up to the final instant in which she felt her own heart stop beating. Madeleine died with her eyes still wide open.

Murphy stood looking down at her still form for a long time, his heart pounding. Finally, he bent down and lifted her into a reclining position on the settee. Taking her arms one at a time, he crossed them across her chest, in the classic posture of the dead hero.

He knelt down, touching her hair and face with his fingertips, feeling the soft, warm texture of her skin. Then, bending lower, he pressed his cheek against hers, testing her body temperature with a little shiver of excitement. Soon, very soon now, she would be cold enough. He kissed her still lips briefly and stood up. He headed for the bathroom to wash and shave and tidy his hair. Madeleine would want him to look his best when they made love.

DC Reid was already waiting outside Murphy's house as Taggart and Jardine arrived, having responded instantly to the request over the car radio.

'Thanks for meeting us,' Taggart said. 'There's probably a girl with him — she might need a woman's sympathy.'

Jackie Reid nodded towards the house, where the light from the lounge could clearly be seen. 'Well, Murphy's definitely in. Is he the one?'

'Probably,' Taggart said grimly. He paused for a split second, finally qualifying his answer with a curt nod of the head. 'Yes, he's the one.'

He began to lead the way up the garden path towards the front door.

Murphy slowly and lovingly unpicked the buttons of Madeleine's blouse, exposing the swelling tops of her young breasts and the flimsy lace of her brassiere. He touched the soft, firm flesh with his fingertips, running them down the shallow valley between her breasts until they reached the frontal fastening of the bra. Breathing heavily, with mounting excitement, he unpicked the simple clip and pulled the brassiere apart.

Murphy feasted his eyes on Madeleine's creamy breasts for a few delicious moments. Then, licking his lips with anticipation, he began to lower his face towards them.

The loud shrill of the doorbell sliced through the silence. Murphy jumped, his head whirling towards the door, the adrenaline pumping through his system. He got to his feet quickly, crossing the room to the window and pulling back the curtains a few inches. He recognised Taggart as he pressed the doorbell for the second time.

Murphy hurried back to Madeleine's body and grasped her by the feet. He began to drag the corpse across the carpet towards the hallway. Pausing at the foot of the stairs, he released Madeleine's feet and dropped to his knees, pulling up a section of the carpet and exposing the trapdoor of the cellar beneath. He pulled the flap up and rose to his feet again, dragging the corpse to the mouth of the trapdoor and stuffing it awkwardly down the flight of wooden steps which led down to the cellar. Finally, he slid down the steps on his bottom behind her and closed the trap above his head, taking care to pull the carpet back into place above it.

The cellar was dark but for a faint yellow glow from the heated vivarium which housed the remaining stolen snakes. Murphy wriggled into position on the steps and waited, his heart pounding.

The seconds ticked away. The doorbell rang again, and then there was another pause. Finally, Murphy heard the muffled sound of breaking glass and splintering wood as Taggart and Jardine forced their way into the house.

Hardly daring to breathe, Murphy listened to the dull thud of footsteps and the faint creak of floorboards above his head as Taggart, Jardine and Jackie Reid searched the house.

It seemed to go on forever. The sound of footsteps approached, receded, then returned again. Cupboards were opened, drawers were pulled out, doors opened and closed. Occasionally Murphy heard the faint mutter of conversation, too indistinct for him to know what was actually being said.

Finally, there was a long period of silence. Murphy continued to wait, not daring to believe that they had actually gone away. His eyes had begun to adjust to the gloom. He looked down at Madeleine's body sprawled, head down, across the steps beneath him. Her wide-open eyes stared up at him accusingly, their lifeless, glistening irises reflecting the faint glow of light from the vivarium.

Even as he stared, a large, hairy house spider dropped from the ceiling above on to her face, scuttled across to her breasts and began to run up her body towards him.

Murphy reacted involuntarily, kicking out at the corpse in a reflex gesture of horror. The body rolled away from his foot and dropped down the four remaining steps to the cellar floor. Madeleine's shoes clacked loudly against the wooden steps, the noise amplified by the echoing confines of the cellar walls.

Above the pounding of his heart and the pulsing of blood in his head, Murphy heard the sound of footsteps above him once again. They stopped, directly above his head, and there was a brief babble of voices.

Then the sound of the trapdoor being opened and the sudden shock of light streaming on to his face.

Taggart's eyes took in the frightened, crouching young man and the crumpled body of Madeleine lying on the cellar floor. 'Aw, no,' he said, in helpless protest. He began to ease himself down through the trapdoor towards the cowering Murphy.

Chapter Twenty-six

Colin Murphy lolled back in his chair, looking calm and relaxed. There was a distant smile on his face, as if recalling some fond memory.

Taggart sat opposite him, hunched and tense in his own chair, while Jardine sat on the desk between them, his fingers poised above the controls of the tape recorder. It had been a long, harrowing interview session for both of them. No matter how one became inured to the horrors of the job, there was really nothing to prepare for a descent into the sick and twisted world of the necrophiliac.

'They have to be dead, you see,' Murphy was saying, for perhaps the twentieth time. 'They're so beautiful, so peaceful, when they're dead. I thought of using cobra venom — injecting it into the belly-button — but it's how you get them to lie still that's the problem.' He looked up at Jardine, grinning. 'I still don't know if it would work.'

Jardine's face was grim. He glanced across at Taggart, who gave him a curt, weary nod. Jardine picked up the tape recorder microphone on its stand and held it to his mouth.

'This is Detective Sergeant Michael Jardine concluding the interview with Colin Murphy at ten forty-three on the night of Thursday, the first of February, which took place within Interview Room Number Four at Maryhill Police Station.'

He switched off the tape recorder, pressing the bell on the side of the desk. The door opened, and two uniformed officers stepped in to the room to escort Murphy away.

Taggart uncoiled himself from his chair, placing himself directly in line with Murphy as he was escorted to the door. He stood facing the young man, his face hard and grim.

'The mother of one of your victims took her own life today,' Taggart said coldly, staring Murphy directly in the eyes. 'And you know something? I'm glad. I'm glad that she never had to know what kind of . . .'

Taggart's voice broke as he tailed off in mid-sentence, unable to continue. He jerked his head away so that Murphy and the two police officers would not see the tears welling up in his eyes. He turned his body, taking a step away, trying to force himself to control the rage which was building up beneath the sorrow.

It would not be quelled. Despite all his efforts at self-control, Taggart felt something snap inside him. In a sudden, savage explosion of pure hate, he pivoted on the ball of one foot and whirled about, his arm lashing out.

The back of Taggart's hand smashed into Murphy's face, splitting open his top lip and drawing blood. Without looking to see what damage the blow had caused, Taggart dropped his head in shame and strode out of the room without another word. Outside, in the corridor, he stopped, staring blankly out through the window.

Jardine stepped up behind him. 'I think we could do with a drink, sir,' he suggested quietly.

Taggart turned slowly, his face calmer. 'I hit him, Michael,' he muttered. 'I wanted to kill him, God help me.'

Jardine gave a philosophical smile. 'Maybe it's not us that needs the help.'

Taggart nodded, slowly and thoughtfully. 'Sometimes I wonder, Mike,' he observed. 'Sometimes I wonder.'